ALLNIGHTER

PULP FACTION > PO BOX 12171 > LONDON > N19 3HB
http://www.pulpfact.demon.co.uk

First published 1997 by Pulp Faction
Copyright © Pulp Faction, 1997
All rights reserved,
including the right to reproduce
this book or portions thereof
in any form whatsoever.
Permission must be obtained for the
reproduction of any item.
Printed in England.
British Library CIP data: available
from the British Library
ISBN: 1899571051

Editor: Michael River
Assistant Editors: Elaine Palmer, Robyn Conway
Cover design: Engine
Page design: Michael River
Photo credits: 23 Marc Atkins
24,28 Julia King
30-33 Craig Yamey
40,46,54 P-P Hartnett
56,69,109 Elaine Palmer
Distributors UK: Central Books 0181 986 4854
Website: http://www.pulpfact.demon.co.uk
Thanks to: Richard Moss, Gethyn, London Arts Board, Red Devil, Virgin Megastores and all the writers and artists who have contributed to Pulp Faction.

Contents

Interference	Emma Payne	4
Living with raptors	Iain Sinclair	8
Airport '89	Jamie Jackson	24
Jimmy No-nose	Nicholas Blincoe	30
Litter	Carol Swain	35
The gangster's finger	Kirk Lake	40
German Fokker	Tim Etchells	46
Westend	Emma Payne	54
Outcaste	Jacqueline Lucas	56
Super powers on sunday night	Niven Govinden	63
Stars in her eyes	Amy Prior	68
Blood sugar	AD Atkins	76
Nightswimming	Jonathan Gibbs	82
Judgment night	Joe Ambrose	90
Yung liver	Adam j Maynard	104
Through the looking glass	Elinor Hodgson	106
Lisa drives home	Alistair Gentry	109
Snowbaby	Catherine Johnson	117
Humanly impossible rhythms	Sophie	122
Perpetual dawn	Charlie Crafford	124

Once her nights exploded regularly with the racket, two-door thumps of couples coming home, arguing out of the car and into the one-door slam of their houses, white noise of leaves when it rained and bike tyres rustling along the pavement. Her last house it was like making your bed in the road some nights, dogshit on the sheets, fag butts between your toes, a gutter river running through it.

Only little birds tweeting up here, whirr of pumps and fans inside aeroplane engines. A lump of blue ice teetering ready to fall through the roof above, aerosol can hissing in the flat below ready to blast up through the ceiling.

> She folds herself into her bed with the sheets. She used to hear the TV from next door—"Did he, is he... dead?" Sometimes small, flat rows—"You always say this, and every time it's the same thing..."

>> Up here there are thick carpets, thick curtains and puffy soft furnishings which suck up outside interference.

>>> Even when the pub next door was quiet, that was worse, as if they were all sitting in the dark with their fingers to their lips, holding back a mass giggle. Still it's a pillow over the head, to drown out the crackle of the water in the pipes. Every time she thinks she's going off, they give an intestinal gurgle, as someone else stands scratching by the sink filling a glass.

Down near the bottom of the bed, under sheets and blankets and pillows, it's definitely a haven. Except for the scratching under the bed, sounds like perhaps a huge cockroach rubbing its mandibles together, gleefully eating her dead skin.

It starts with listening to the industrial hum of the world turning on its axis and the rumble of lorries on the motorways, and then you're hearing the zoom of vehicles left and right on the A roads, and motorbikes turning the corners on B roads, and pushbikes coming to a halt in cul-de-sacs, and then you can hear gears changing and clutches brought clumsily up, and the pulleys in the lift shaft screaming with the strain, and the pigeons in the roof clattering their feet, and the creak of joists above and the window resettling in its groove, and the click of key wards in bolts and little latches and the rattle of your bed with the echo of others' settling down, and the stillness of your bed but the rattle of something which is your kidneys washing out some waste and the slither of saliva running down your throat and the oiling of your eyeballs and the crackle of the lashes and the chatter of bacteria, and then you know there is never going to be enough peace to sleep.

Emma Payne is working on a novel about her experiences in military intelligence.

Passion is always difficult. Writing about it in retrospect, when the damage has been done, and the immune system circumvented. Pytchley was dizzy; each step on the damp grass a test of memory. He lurched, stretched out his free hand, felt for a solid object to break his fall. The ground was untrustworthy. He was a revenant in his own park.

living with
or, the missionary

That's what being away from London did. Travel disorientated him. The return home was the worst journey in the world. But, in his present condition, there was nowhere he would rather be, the bosom of his family, the chatter of his daughters. Webs of bird-spit glittered in the trees, delicate traceries provoking quietly erotic seizures. Country itches: the frottage of uncircumcised cockhead on muddy corduroy. The drench of horse-droppings on tarmac, steaming industrial slurry. Where better to initiate a slow convalescence?

iain sinclair

raptors
position

The perfect recluse. The suicide who is still alive.
—Peter Whitehead

It was confusing, those lost hours, not knowing who he was, what mask he should adopt. Coming back out of the black hole, the little death of anaesthesia. Like sex, he thought, you never return to the same body. He'd watched the dance of candlelight, backs broken, bent to one shape; watched himself, watched his partner; seen himself through her eyes; herself through his. He'd hovered and he'd swooped. Thrashed, branded. Licked the lush, suppurating wounds as if they were his own. Who *was* he now? This early morning walk would not settle it. Peter Pytchley: author, dramaturge, collector of curiosa, Egyptologist? Or Alan Wolfehead: Secret State spook, fixer, psychic hitman? "Pete the Porn" or "The Falconer"? Village shaman? Art gigolo? High Arctic adventurer? Dope smuggler? Shape-shifter? Elective gentleman? Pytchley, Wolfehead. Wolfehead, Pytchley. The names echoed and reechoed to the spike and suck of his shooting stick, the drag of his dead heel. Guilty of everything. Nameless. Conscious of nothing beyond this circumference of pain.

The countryside was so loud: the whine of traffic, out on the arterial road, hurtling back to town. The carcinogenic singe of electricity swooping through the cradle of high voltage wires. Shotguns bringing down rooks. Man-traps. Chattering gossips. There were no buildings to buffer these inane interferences, to blanket his annoyance. The silence, out here, was rapacious. It fed on the hurt of his breath, the febrile hammering of his heart. No time left. Time marching through the repaired chambers like squadrons of Edgar Allan Poe gold bugs.

"I'm lost," he muttered, "my soul has drawn back to its virginity." Unearthed on goat-cropped lawns, he sweated sharp crystals of fear. Disembodied in the sting of post-operative replays, he couldn't keep the night-thoughts in their cage. Sounds from the cutting room, chance remarks, a running tap. How they invoke the grind of the drill, the saw splintering dry bone. The cracking of ribs.

He walked, he limped. Where was he? There wasn't another property in sight. He could have been anywhere. That was his choice, his preferred life style. His wife, an artist, preoccupied with her own work. The current mistress straining at the barre. Or scoring a Voodoo jigjig. Nocturnals. Evening people. People who kept to their delegated quarters, meeting only for meals in the spacious, light-dappled kitchen. Meals that his wife would prepare. Francophile social arrangements on a pre-revolutionary Russian estate. *The Cherry Orchard* revamped by L.F. Céline. That's how he thought of it. As he hammered at the Bechstein grand. Sombre fugues of his own composition. God, he had magnificent hair. From blond to silver overnight. The traumas of genius. The agony of stalled composition.

Eyes cold as stone. Skin like under-franked papyrus. Trembling hand. When no one watched him, his fires died. His shoulder dipped beneath a burden of remembered feathers. Bird-come running from the brim of his curious black hat. The curse of intelligence: seeing the multiverse as it really was. The energy fields, the rigorous elegance of scientific description. Systems of disbelief. His project? To stay alive and stay sane. *Stay* sane?

No more hallucinations, extended sick leave. No chemical forcing, no dubious mushrooms. The dream was as valid as any other part of the script. An equal, not an alternate, reality. This morning air, the sound of snail shells crunched by the beaks of thrushes, was his fantasy. English ground. Mellow brick, thatch, Virginia creeper. Cats stalking small vermin. A brain-damaged lurcher banging its snout against a dry stone wall. Boots that spilled desert sand. Pytchley had the soul of a Bedouin. And most of the *Oxford Book of English Verse* by heart. Yeats, Hopkins. Fellow birdmen. And Francis Thompson. The city would never leave him while he had the puff to recreate Thompson's morbid labyrinth.

His task? To balance the millennial elements, narcissism and melancholy. The troubled silence of drowned fields. Lamplight in his wife's workroom. The established English are so good at avoiding each other. He walked, letting the fugitive sentences take form. Like Henry James in Lamb House, with his oval circuit, one turn of the walled garden, lawn to amphitheatre to stable-block, a long-breath paragraph. Like James, the hesitation, the sleeve brushed across the eye, at the pets' graveyard. The empty falcon cages. The breeding pens. He staggered, his bowed legs spearing the wet grass like a pair of bent compasses.

The strength went out of him. He rested on a broken pillar. And saw— the old eidetic faculty was still active—the startling carmine lips of a Vargas pin-up floating in the green depths of a box hedge. Lips to inspire a Dali sofa. Lips that could shovel snow. A resting sex muscle, a labial erection. Wet, pouting, unsatisfied. Cartoon rinds so pumped with collagen invitation it was an offence not to dive straight into them, head first. And the teeth? White as shock, the afterburn of skull-bursting migraines. White as absence, nothingness. The impossible pearl dazzle of hyper-real adverts, where time implodes. And eternities are exhausted in a scatter of over-active microseconds. Computer generated claps of the eye.

Pytchley, a trained physicist, was impressed by the demonstration. Or, more properly, expressed by it. Self-demonstrated to an extent that made it impossible for him to move. He had two shooting-sticks to cope with. His eyes had fused into a single stalk—which threatened to split its socket. He had not thought himself capable of this. Not in his present state, the touch of embalming fluid still potent in his veins. It's strange when your thighs have been rerouted to your heart. You don't know if you're hiking or peddling frantically to circulate lethargic blood. Each step is a lung-bursting orgasm. Each orgasm an explosion of black feathers. For years Pytchley had rehearsed, revised, his suicide scene. In the desert, in a mud hut in Pakistan, the Outer Isles—fending off demons with a falcon lure. The whistle of a decapitated pigeon whirled on a thong. He had written himself into pyramid chambers and unexplored spaces within crystals. He had died and died again. The dry retch of mescaline. Now this. This scarlet surge. The Dionysiac purification of sight.

"Hi, I'm Tronna. You don't know me. Not yet. But, mister, I sure know you."

A voice from the bush. The grating shriek of the Mid-West. Corn-fed innocence. Poisonous milk shakes. Pure James: American virtue offering itself to the dust tongue of Europe. A necrophile embrace underwritten by pillows of sweet-smelling, hay-breathed cash. Pytchley was all too familiar with that scenario. But what was the bint doing in his garden? (Tronna had her own reservations. Fucking the spook would be like falling into a vat of discarded bandages. Spooning locusts. Being blindfolded while a warty toad was placed on the tongue.)

From the voice, Pytchley, an old pro, read the rest: the compulsory, shoulder-length peroxide swarm, the doughy bosom and the short legs. He could taste pink toxins of bubble-gum. Such creatures, in truth, were outside his experience. He modelled this materialised wet dream on playbacks of Hank Janson (who he had never read).

Trouble was, the woman was doing an equal job on him. The silver-tongued, hawk-profiled English gent. An Englishness that could only be achieved by Low Scots, potato-bashers and too cultivated Hungarian Jews. Pytchley came from the era before all Hollywood Englishmen were sadists, culture Nazis. Tronna had the bite, the steam, that the neurasthenic dilettante lacked. The vampire in him sniffed her shoes.

He was unsurprised, incapable of it. He rewrote the world, on the spur, to accommodate uncanny, ill-disciplined showers of blood, fireballs over ancient stone circles, brown bathwater. "Ah yes, *I* did that." A terrible burden for anyone to bear. Holographic consciousness. Self and double. So she, this creature stepping forward, tottering on absurd heels, was an avatar of all the others. The glamour girls, strippers, dancers. He had summoned her, this lacquered initiator of onanism. A dragged-up masquerade of his anima, his female part.

You have to be properly incarnated before you can be reincarnated. He prepared himself for absorption by this advancing mass, the harlot-madonna in the lurid raincoat. So extreme was the punning self-parody of the Scarlet Woman that the beast in him suspected a Divine Director with a sense of humour. Colour so eager and shiny that it poked a finger in his eye. The red wrap arrived, creaking at every wiggle, seconds ahead of the creature who modelled it. Inky eyelashes curled into questions, sixes, Crowleyesque signatures.

"You the guy screws crows?"

That voice again. Rats in a blender. Car alarms parroting mandarin. He twitched as she thrust a gilded magazine into his face. A puff, a gloriously overwritten profile. Pytchley and his women, his falcons. His obituary.

"Says here you co-pu-late with guy falcons and finger fuck the chicks."

"That's gyr, pronounced 'jur'. Gyr falcons. The most precious and sacred birds in the natural world. And, yes, the males express over my hat and my boots. And I introduce their semen, on my fingers, into the vulvas of receptive females."

"Gross. That is truly gross. Can you show me?" Tronna hoisted a scarlet camera. A scream of plastic that matched her raincoat and her painted talons.

"Please." But it was too late. The flash blinded him.

"Sorry, Pete. That's for definition. Get some life into your face. This country is just so godawful, pardon me, grim. Like the lights are out, period."

What Tronna was after was the godlike beauty of Alan Wolfehead, Pytchley's earlier self—as revealed in this magazine plant. A full-page spread, hawk on wrist, mistress at shoulder.

"I had to come, Pete. As soon as I touched those pages. You were the living seed of Jesus."

Tronna, clutching his arm and dragging him back towards the sanctuary of the house, the open doors of the kitchen, gifted him with the story of her life. Unexpurgated, uncut. Triumphs and tears. He was her trophy, all that silver-mint hair. She wanted to carry him back to Mom in a picnic basket. The bleeding head of John the Baptist. And in exchange? She whispered in his ear. There was no between. She shouted like a cattle boss or she tried for girly and coy, breathless with naughtiness. When he filmed her, he'd have to find a way to make sure she kept her mouth shut. The banality had him blushing for shame, that he was capable of such an ugly fantasy. Because there was no way he would accept that this could be happening. Not to Peter Pytchley. Not in the English countryside as he knew it.

She'd crossed the pond as a tambourine smacker. From Salt Lake City or wherever. A god whore to one of those Orals. A come-on girl backing a margarine-haired messiah. A door-stepper. A light-in-the-eyes, tingle-in-your-lap babe. A "yea" sayer. Tough as teak. If you didn't convert, sign over your tithe, she'd beat your brains out with her bible. A many times, born-again virgin.

Wolfehead, as she read about him, cried out for saving. Dragging down to the river. That boy had the emaciated body, the holy mane of the crucified Christ. And, in the Lord's name, she was going to nail him. She wasn't so sure about the transmogrified form, this Pytchley. More like punctured salvage from the tree. Holes in the palms of his hands. The whiff of the cave still seeping from his oxters. But his voice—oh, oh, that voice!—it had her purring like a coyote on heat in a truckstop corral.

Pytchley, liking the sounds her coat made, the protective shell of the woman, had no such problems. Daughter. One of his daughters. From the West Coast trip, surely? After that little misunderstanding with Orson Welles. The restaurant tab that was still in dispute. He might forget what the mothers looked like, but all his women fell into two types: artists and dancers. Sculptors who took themselves off out of it, to their capacious studios. Slim stunners who photographed alabaster heads in museum basements. Object makers with a private income. And then they were the ballet girls, the Isadora Duncan types who could work up a death dance from a tape of his jazz-funk music. Exhibitionists who anticipated his every whim. Chicks who spread their own cheeks. Soho casuals whacked out in drug-dependency clinics and unreconstructed Northampton madhouses.

Tronna, as she admitted with a simper, *had* been a kind of dancer once, before she was saved. Exotic. Laptop. The kind of gal politicians and movers went for. That Clinton, why, he'd had so many complimentary blow jobs he looked like an inflatable. Like Ronald McDonald.

Excellent. Pytchley, testing her with his full weight, had found his latest blonde. There had been so many. And all the same. He spoke of the double helix, the caduceus, spiral galaxies. How he has assisted Crick, tutored Sheldrake, penetrated the mysteries of X-ray crystallography. He helped her hand towards the lump in his pocket, the blood-red stone he was never without. "But we'll speak of these matters another time, my dear. We have used enough of my vigour for today."

Passion's difficult, I guess. But this Englishman is one strange hombre, know what I'm saying? That voice. It comes right at you—like Sir Anthony Hopkins. Remember? Hannibal Lecter, down there in the slammer, when he just knows what scent Jodie's dabbed on, how she's dripping with fear and whatever. He can snort yesterday's panties. Well, this Pytchley guy's like that. He understands, umm, right where you live. Spooky, but kind of sexy too.

And his hair! I want it. I want to take a bath in that stuff. It's long like a faggot rock star and it shines, and you can, umm, tell he's never had to work the streets in his entire life. His hands are smooth as a baby, a sex killer. Taking a cab out of town was the best move I ever made. It is passion, kind of. Obsession, anyhow. I gotta have him. Get him on film. I believe that. I do. I have witnessed the light. And he's made of it.

I wouldn't let him know it, but I could just eat him alive. Gobble him up. I swear I could. But I have to take it slow, real easy. Can't scare him. Let him talk and talk and talk. Talk himself right out. Talk out the devil and come on back to the arms of Jesus. The joy of the sinner that repenteth. And he's going to repent, baby, repent until he dies of it.

I'm wet. He's got me so wet I'm splashing the bathroom floor. I can hear him, right from the little girl's room. He won't stop talking. I want to sit on his face. That evil, holy voice. A shower of silver coins falling into the deacon's dish.

His aura was remarkable, a purple nimbus flickering to blue. Cold. The man was ice. She watched him openly, without disguise. He had stayed in control, he was driving. But so slowly. Taking such care. As if any movement of the wheel threatened to tear out the platinum stitches of his heart. And light flooded over them both. Now he saw her, now she was gone. Reds and golds and silvers. The nightworld of the road. She had persuaded him back to London.

This was a mistake, a kind of death. A reincarnation as Wolfehead, as state approved hack, double agent. Instrument of fate. The capsule of the car was not moving, the world moved gently against it. Now Tronna talked, rested her hand, for emphasis, on his knee. She became, in that warm darkness, the dancer. He listened, sympathised, entered her narrative. Shared it. Provoked it. He was Tronna. Himself, herself. The old man,

Tiresias, in exile as a temple prostitute.

She was stroking him through the tweed. Yes, Wolfehead rising. American women smelt different. Soaped, showered, shaved. And the meat under it. The sweetness of the meat. She was hot in her plastic. He was collaborating in a ritual suicide. Whatever he thought, in the hallucination of the on-coming headlights, became the script. He tightened his grip. Kept his speed to a rigid 40 miles per hour. Did his breathing. The landscape was hunched and submissive, sliding him back to his earlier self, the pre-heart attack metropolitan. The man who squired Arabs around gambling clubs. The chronicler of the counter-culture. The spy, the manipulator. The energy thief. The dude who *really* made those stag movies. The Donald Cammell to Chris Petit's Nicolas Roeg.

He wasn't familiar with the east side. He'd always said that he was. Connected. Running with the gangs. On terms. But that was part of the front. He was lost. He could have been in Moscow. She worked him. Guided him through this wilderness of scrub-woods, snuff ponds, ethnics, grease caffs. He had died again. On the slab. Lea Bridge Road, that channel between the living and the immortal dead. The straightened labyrinth with its waxwork guardians.

Conjugations of stars—the night was crisp and sharp—shifted from pub sign to windscreen. And back again. The Pleiades. He remembered, invented, an earlier death plan: in a secret pyramid chamber. Essence into starlight. As she made him drive the dusty vehicle into a car wash. Black men who didn't have the language. White teeth. Scrubbing and hoovering. Tubes and soft yellow cloths. Big brushes blocking it all out. A rush and swoosh of water jets. Tropical rain. Not driving now. The car sliding forward of its own volition.

She takes him in her mouth. Everything scoured, made clean. Polished. He gushes milk into her open hand.

Everyone says Hoxton is one of the sharpest districts in which to live. Well, anyhow, I do. I say it. And I ought to know, I've been here for almost three weeks now. The London *Evening Standard* says so too, because I've got this article cut out and framed on my wall. Hoxton is like, umm, SoHo used to be. Artists and lofts and all kinds of native crafts and industries. They got delis and bars that open for breakfast, and clubs, and it's real close to the St Paul's church and the river and all that stuff... I've never actually lived in New York City, but this is as close as you can come. The smart designers and fashion models on bicycles and pavement cafes with poets. Pete's never been down in these slums, so I got the whip hand. It's my turf.

Now, I've got a teensy confession to make. I'm working on a screenplay. And, yeah, it's kinda based on my own experiences. And, boy, have I had some. Pete, he fits into this, real neat. I'm not expecting to hook some big movie deal, not out of the blue. Not first time. I'm writing it, if you want to know, to see how the story turns out. To see what happens to me, what the future is going to bring. 'Cos Pete explained that all writing is prophecy. You get it straight and it's bound to happen. Words have a kind of magic.

So, I shape what went down, make it over, recall it the best way I can, and this voice takes charge. Not me. The voice of the story. I can just barely keep up when it hits its stride. I'm in it. Pete's in it. Sometimes, umm, his wife, I guess. Real elegant. Beautiful long, high class legs. French or European, right? Waxed not shaved. She digs me. She's a pure delight to know.

Hold on. I'll tell the story. Then it will happen. It has happened. It's happening now. I'm helping Pete up the stairs. I've caught him. He doesn't know where he is or what he's doing. He's lost the script.

How would I cast the picture? Gabriel Byrne, he could play Pete—but not as well, you bet, as Pete would do himself. I mean, Pete's such a natural aristocrat. So gracious and intelligent and fine spoken. Gabriel's good, but he's Irish. And too much of a hunk. Pete's appeal is more subtle. Like you can tell he always knows just what you're going to say, what you're thinking. All the real blushful stuff.

A younger Madonna would be good for my role, but it's too late now, with the baby and all, for that. I'll have to play it myself. See where it goes.

The loft she had was perfect. Quite surprising. It would have surprised a less informed intelligence. Not Pytchley. The black walls. The framed photographs. Polished glass to reflect the viewer. To marry voyeur and object of desire. The spook had been here before, many, many times. It was his set, the interior of the dark crystal, the Egyptian tomb. It was where he played out his psycho dramas, where he released his demons from the aether. Where he contacted the spirit of the bird, of Horus. Where he returned to himself after a liberating voyage through time and space. Where he made sacrifice.

He was tired. The drive had drained him. He allowed himself to be led across the shining floor to the great brass bed. He subsided, saw himself doubled, reversed. A floating other trapped in the bordello mirror. Wolfehead floated over Pytchley. It was too much. Heart pounding. The operation had been botched, something alien left in the wound. He was dying again. Tipping backwards into darkness, spilling his lifeforce. Into the feathers. Into sleep.

Whap! The flashbulb was so close it scorched his eyebrows. She was at it again, logging him. He thrust out his jaw, ironed the folds in his neck. Tossed his hair. She bent forward, a puff of talcum powder, the soothing touch of her hand. So warm. As she slipped the blindfold over his weary eyes. Angel of Death. Healer, killer. Agent of release.

"I'm being raped by images," Pytchley thought. TV replays, barbecued monks. Napalm. Assassination. He went for the big stuff. As he heard the bulbs pop, he conjured up waterfalls that blew back over sheer cliffs. The oldest rocks in the world. Deserts that stretched forever in the mind. Volcanoes. Drifts of bombs. Torched ghettoes. "Images must become instantly forgettable, or we will all go mad! We are conditioned to be blind." In his nightmare, he was unpicked. Layer by layer, print by print. The more she discovered, the less he knew. She cuffed his wrists to the bedhead. "Who am I?" he screamed.

He had the cutest scar you've ever seen. A Nile, a relief river, running straight down his chest and most of the way across his firm belly. Not a hair to be found. Still shaved from the operation and not grown back. But he had, as she discovered, uncoupling his suspenders, shaking him out of his trousers, something else—a curious chastity belt, a corset. Around his waist was this off-white, sweat-stained, shamanistic, Joseph Beuys garment.

What was its purpose? She ran her hands over the porous material. Was it something to do with his operation? Did it hold him together? There were pouches sewn into the belt, big enough to carry limestone pebbles, or bullion bars. Phials of drugs. Microfilms.

"My eggs. Don't touch my eggs." He surfaced from his reverie, heard himself speak. The woman was fiddling with his egg belt, trying to find the catch. Pytchley as an incubator of falcons. Pytchley travelling back from Iceland or Morocco. His associates always spoke of his "cool". Nothing phased him. He breezed through border posts. The belt was his pregnancy wrap, he mothered birds that he had also sired. Father and mother, both. Eggs, in a cheesy belt, held against the warmth of his belly. Like the skin, a sculptor once told him, of a man who has been turned inside out. Globules of fat decorating the peeled cast. Eggs of body sweat. Glistening lard trophies.

Blindfolded, Pytchley saw—imagined—too much. Tronna became his Antigone. The old myths are the best myths. Leading him to his doom, favourite daughter. "I am your eyes, Daddy. I have come to guide you through the abandonment of the city." Blindness excusing the incest prohibition. Blindness letting him see. The thongs she had on his wrists and ankles became, perversely, the instruments of his freedom. Not responsible, he could respond. Control, direct. Unable to move, he would inspire movement in others.

He'd expected the cuffs of a nurse's uniform, not the black of a nun. He was back in the hospital, Arabs setting their fires in the corridors. Tethered goats. Not incense and angel music. Wrong tape. The adhesive she was fixing over his mouth. He's trussed like a chicken.

Photographs. It had to be done in photographs. I saw Pete as a book first, then, who knows, if I got lucky, a major exhibition. Somewhere like, oh, that Slaughterhouse Gallery place, down in Smithfield, the old meat market. Berkoff had shown there and plenty of other celebrities. You could, maybe, have the prints upstairs, all along the wall, in sequence—and then you'd be lead to the brink, to where you look over the abyss, down into the cellars. And a spotlight would pick, out of the darkness, Pete's skin hanging on a hook. Early days, but something like that, you know, could be pretty dramatic.

He's likes showing himself, you can tell. He's got plenty to show, he's in shape for an old guy. Flash! I do an establishing shot. The torso. All of it. I'll leave him for now with those white stockings. Surgical supports, I guess, where they took the veins to use in his heart. But the legs are good and if I can arrange them properly, he'll come over kind of kinky, transsexual. Flash! One more from the other side.

I taste the skin of his shoulder. Cold as death. I want to trace all those wounds with my lips. Map him. Flash! An icon. One of the martyred saints. The ridges of his scars are physical features in an undiscovered city. A mysterious continent seen from space. Get right in on those puncture holes. Flash! Whatever I frame changes the fate of the city. He has to live up to these beautiful prints. And by dying again, if that's what it takes.

From the street you could see the pulsing window. The instants of illumination. The woman moving backwards and forwards against the uncurtained rectangle. A frame of cinema. And with each starburst, Pytchley sank deeper into his trance,

21

willed her on, solicited the prick of the blade. The slashes that would heal his wounds by re-opening them. He was back at the point of the first attack, crawling towards a glass telephone. His hand reaching out for it. He was there as the first beams of sunlight crept over the lip of the balcony, the trees in the park. The returned suicide. The dead man who has crawled out of the river.

Tronna stood over, stood back, walked around the bed. It was uncanny how the body absorbed light. Pytchley shone like an extra-terrestrial, a starman. It was as if each photograph punctured his carapace, let his spirit flood out. Every image had undone one block of the narrative. He was forgetting his story, escaping the tyranny of remembrance. Bound tight, wrapped like a parcel, he was a pupa. Between larva and imago. A shell secreted out of his own essence. An egg.

Pytchley couldn't have written it better. The brilliance of the lamps. He could see through the black cloth. How Tronna climbed up on to the bed, straddled him. The dead Osiris brought back to life by the hawk. Glamorous, necrophile. A sarcophagus Polaroid. What he'd always wanted, didn't they all? All men. To be mastered, forgiven.

What an unusual name, Tronna. He tried to speak it aloud, test its meaning. She pressed her lips against the vibrating tape. "Not Tronna, honey. Tronno. T-r-o-n-n-o." The letters burnt into his lids. They twitched and danced. Tronno. An androgynous being from a distant galaxy. From some downriver midden. The letters rearranged themselves into a more conventional form. A sound like London. Norton. His oldest enemy in her newest form.

Her hands tore at the cicatrix, the zipper of flesh. Reaching for the wet heart, the falcon. The light from the dark star. Empty pages. Human vellum. The last sentence swallowed in a gush of salt.

Iain Sinclair, a London obsessive, has recently published _Lights Out for the Territory_, a book that documents some of his stranger, off-piste journeys. Previous excursions include _Lud Heat_ & _Downriver_. The material exploited in this story is drawn from a film (_The Falconer_) currently being made with Chris Petit. Posthumous dreams, millennial weather, cardiac arrest, Peter Whitehead, Carolyn Cassady, Francis Stuart, Stewart Home. The usual suspects.

as I walked through Soho, the rain sprayed off the pavements up and at me, sloshing my coat and kicking into my face. I love the rain, the transformation of the world into your very own outdoor bedroom, cosy as fuck, you don't need wallpaper and your mum can't catch you wanking; I could feel it hugging me as I hit Rupert Street, looking for Queenie. rumour had it that he knew where it was, fuck knows no one else did. I must've searched the whole of London for it; Wood Allen's finest hour but the bugger wasn't coming out to play with me. he knows about market forces, the making of legends: keep yourself scarce and you reach mythical status; but I've got to have it, and I can feel the Thames like a snake below, grinning, flashing its teeth through the fog as the night starts biting and I cruise into the heart of Soho. by night it's a neon jungle. the sleaze shops are doing their trade diligently, but it's the strip joints and nude bars which are dazzling the rain into silver bullets as they bang and rip my face; just the way I like it.

jamie jackson

airport '89

I pass a couple, looking at the women. most are rough as fuck, but there is the odd light that never goes out, chewing a fag, trying to entice me in for a blowjob or a pint of lager. that's not for me though, not tonight anyway, not in my current financial state; each'll cost thirty quid of my hard earned dole money and the pint'd definitely last longer.

I stop on the corner of Old Compton Street and Wardour and decide to hit the next strip joint I see and ask around after Queenie. I find one named, originally, Joe's strip bar, so I step out of the street and into it. there's no one around and I need a fag. typical. any other time you walk down here they're grabbing you in. I ring the bell on the counter and wait.

"hello. how can I help you?"

I look around but can't see anyone. then a head pops up from below the counter and I'm face to face with a ten year old boy.

"hello, can I help you?"

"you what?" I'm struggling here, he's the last thing I expected, and now I notice his irritation.

"can I help you?"

"you what?"

"can I help you? 'cos if not you shouldn't have rung the bell." he looks at me badly, like I smell, waiting for my dumb brain to kick into action.

"er... is your mum around?"

"my mum? you've come in here to ask me about my mum!!? Jesus Christ."

the little bastard. what else does he expect, seeing his ugly little mug stuck behind the counter. fuck me, has he no pride? working in a joint like this.

"tell me," he says, brightening a little, "this is something that has been troubling me for a couple of days now. do you feel Oasis are the new Beatles or merely working class Mancs made good?"

I look at him. the little idiot, is he taking the piss? but no, he has a serious and inquisitive look and well, this is something that I do, if I'm at all honest, have the odd opinion on. I look him in the eye and answer, "well, obviously, by the nature of language my reply is bound to be interpreted in a sense that I may not intend or, indeed, desire, but no, in short, Oasis are certainly not the new Beatles. however," I pause for breath, catching sight of a packet of Bensons, which are my favourites, on the counter. "d'you mind if I have one of them, please?"

"sure," he says, and before I say anything more, he's up and kneeling on the counter, shoving a fag in my mouth and fumbling with a lighter that's laying on a couple of old porno mags. he can't get it to work and so he says to me, "have you got one?"

"sure I have," and again before I can say anything, he's jumped off the counter and has his hand in my pocket and is pulling out my lighter, and sparking my fag for me.

"cheers," I say, feeling myself begin to soften a little. "aren't you having one?"

"no, they're bad for your health. I'll stick to these."

he pulls a packet of lollys from his pocket and sticks one in his mouth, and begins sucking on it loudly. it's actually quite disgusting watching him standing there under the red light, the lolly juice beginning to dribble down from his wet lips, glistening in the glow of the phosphorescent beam.

for a strip joint, this isn't fucking turning me on.

"now that we're friends," he says, "maybe we can go out to play." he starts for the open door and the rain that's still hurling down, but having had my share of the fag I spit it out under his feet. he looks at me sternly. "want some of my lolly, do we?"

"no thanks, what I want is Queenie, or more to the point, airport '89. any ideas?"

"Queenie? who the fuck is Queenie?"

"he's a bloke who I've been told knows where airport '89 is."

"what's airport '89?"

at this I have to give him a funny look; I mean, he doesn't know what airport '89 is.

"it's Wood Allen's finest hour. a record. a 12 inch house music all time Blackburn warehouse classic. from 1989. hence the title."

"alright, alright. don't get all fucking snotty about it 'cos I've never heard of it. I was only three years old then, know what I mean?"

there's not much I can say to that, so I concentrate on the

cigarette still burning away on the floor and watch it roll out towards the rain and the dark evening which has swallowed everything else up around me, leaving only the little shit and the hovel we're standing in. I'm conscious of a noise and realise he's waiting for a reply to something.

"what?"

"look," he says, "I told you when you first came in here, if you don't answer me straight then you may as well fuck right off. I said, what d'you want this record for?"

"I'm a DJ aren't I?"

with this news, it's his turn to look at me funny but I take no notice, other people never understand, you know what it's like when you're into something. I'd got used to that look from just about everyone else I'd told.

just then a woman comes in from the back room. she stops at the sight of me and gives me the once over. a slow once over, while I take in her overly rouged lipstick and big gold earrings.

"Cecil," she says, "get in that back room will you, and do that homework like I told you."

"but mum, it's Latin tonight and I can't be arsed... and I've told you not to call me Cesh, haven't I, you old boot."

now she looks at me and suddenly it's me and her against Cecil. she raises her eyebrows and motions her head towards him like she can't believe what he's like.

"what is he like, eh?" she rasps at me, "it's only a bit of Homer, the Odyssey and the one about Icarus. I've told him I'll help him, but you can't do it all, can you love?"

"you certainly can't," I say, delivering my lines rather sheepishly.

"what is it you're after love?"

"Queenie."

"Queenie?"

"yeah."

"yeah, I might know him. come through here with me."

she turns and I follow her, making sure I give a superior smirk to let the boy know who's in charge now. I walk into a back room where three kids sit on a sofa, wearing sunglasses and drinking milk through straws, watching old reruns of test cricket. as I pass directly behind them, they all turn as one, look at me and then turn back again, in complete silence and complete unison. "don't take any notice of them," says my guide. "they're in training for the Atlanta Olympics. they're up in two disciplines for synchronised gold."

"oh. I see."

now we're into the kitchen and some stairs leading downwards. the woman turns to me and says, "right. you want Queenie, yeah?" "yeah, I certainly do," I reply. "c'mon then." she steps onto the stairs. reluctantly, I follow.

as I descend, I begin to worry, but then the thought of airport '89 and the glory it'll bring me when I spin the wheels of steel to all the punters urges me on. when I hit the bottom, it's dark.

I look around slowly. nothing. apart from the sound of... breathing. a rasping sound, like someone choking. but quietly. like they're aware of the protocol in such matters, not wishing to offend.

"put the light on," a voice wheezes.

"I can't."

"why not?"

"I don't know where it is."

"just by your nose."

I look and see it just at the end of my nose, so I lean forward, like you'd do if you were me, in my position, and rub the light on with my nose, FLAAAAASH, on comes a flood of light, and there's Cesh's mum, kneeling on the floor, playing a nintendo.

"behind you!" it's the same voice, the wheeze.

I turn round and see an old man, big bulldog face, fat hanging over his lap as he sits, looking and rasping at me in a wheelchair.

"hello there."

"hello."

"glad to meet you," he says. "my name's Queenie."

I gasp at this, barely able to tell him who I am.

"what can I do for you?"

"I'm, I'm, I'm looking for a record. airport '89, by—"

"—Wood Allen. yes I know it well." he looks at me, the light catching a silver tooth and flashing. "his finest hour, would you not say?"

"yes!"

"come with me then and we'll see what we can do." he takes something from under his seat and tosses it to Cesh's mum. "there you go Matilda. Tetris. top score I've had to date is in the upper regions of two hundred thou. I kid you not. beat it and I'll be surprised." with that he turns and rolls the wheelchair down the small tunnel, leaving tracks in the damp sand I now find myself treading in as I follow him. he disappears into a small room and when I get in there I see it is a small disco area with dancefloor and DJ's booth at one end. on a table is a big cardboard box of records. Queenie is sitting there, holding one in his hand.

"airport '89," he says smiling.

this is it, the end of the holy fucking grail, from Camden to Camberwell and back again, and now I've finally made it. they said I never would, but I'll show them, I'll make a DJ yet. before I can say anything, Queenie's over at the booth, on the decks, switching the whole goddamned sound system on and slapping the disc down.

heaven on earth I can die happy Wood, I love you what a fucking tune

Queenie brings the volume down, creating a silence that is indeed golden.

"tell me," he says, "why do you want this record?"

"why," I ask, incredulous at such an obviously answerable question. "because I'm a DJ."

"really," he says. now it's his turn to look incredulous as he slowly gazes down my shoulders, along my sides. "but you haven't got any arms."

"I know," says I. "so?"

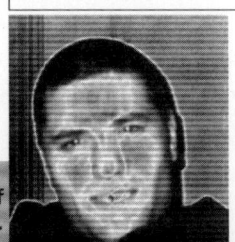

Jamie Jackson writes all his stuff in a darkened room full of skulls.

I'd been away a long time. My first night back I heard this story...

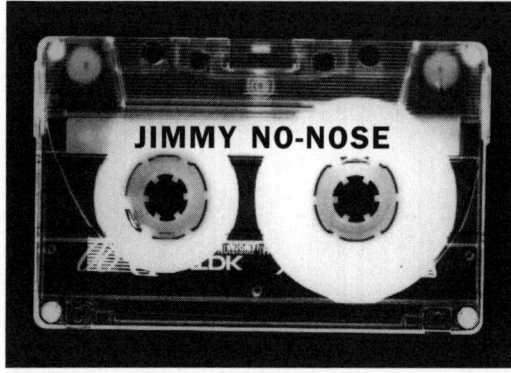

Nicholas BLINCOE

Jimmy No-Nose is a guy who lives on his own up the Bishop Estate. He's old, he's ugly, he's got no job, no family, no nose and he's a heroin addict. But he always says he's the luckiest man in the world. And he tells everyone.

Jimmy's a mechanic. He's hardly had a proper job in fifteen years and he's been a junkie for longer, but whenever he's got himself a stash and bought himself some time there's nothing he likes better than spending the day working on a car. Which is what he was doing this one day. He woke early, took a breakfast injection and lugged his tool kit out to the roadside. Then he slipped under the cracked sump of a wrecked Fiesta and lost track of time.

It wasn't until late in the afternoon that he began to feel the old dull ache in his bones. So he hauls himself upright and stands at the edge of the kerb, shaking out a leg and patting himself down, looking for his cigarettes. When he finds them in the bib of his overalls, he uses his long junkie fingernails to slide one out, trying his best to get as little oil on the cigarette as possible. Standing there, black face and hands, covered in a thick sheet of grease from his head to his knees, he has his smoke but he can't find a lighter. So he marches back into his house, treading oil every step from the front door through to the kitchen. And when he tries to light his cigarette on the stove, whoosh, he goes up in flames.

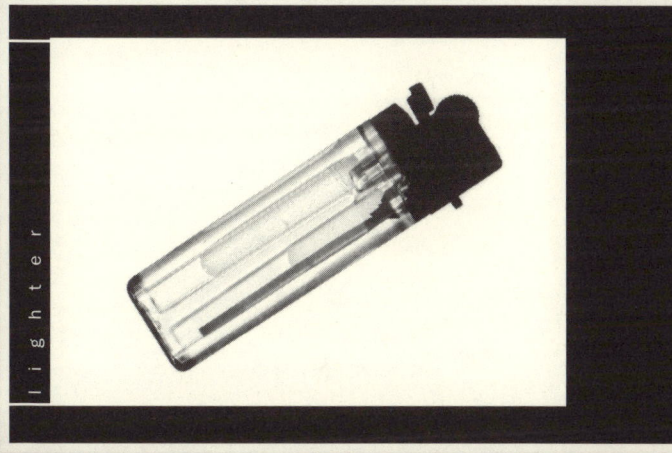

lighter

Jimmy spent two weeks on the critical list before anyone even began to consider reconstructive surgery. The doctors never did manage to build him a respectable new nose so that's how he got his name. But that's only half his story.

The day he was released from hospital, Jimmy hooked up with four old friends and they suggested he do some celebrating. After all the months he'd spent in hospital, Jimmy was looking forward to what a little heroin could do to his de-toxed system. He followed them happily. He even offered to brew the tea while they cooked the gear.

When he came in with the tea, the other four were well away. Jimmy thought, Hey up, I'd better hurry to catch up. The heroin hit him with an almighty rush and it was only as he was beginning to resurface, ready for the last long dive downwards, that he noticed how quiet the other guys were. Doped to the eyeballs, Jimmy still managed to walk amongst them, shaking them and trying to wake them. Then he called for an ambulance and sank into a coma. When he woke back in hospital, he was told he'd escaped death by seconds. The others were gone, taken off by the ninety per cent pure gear they'd injected.

So now Jimmy No-Nose has this mantra: I'm old and ugly, I got no job, no family, no nose and I'm a heroin addict but I'm the luckiest man in the world. Then he tells his story and the story gets passed around and eventually it reached me. To be honest, it was funnier the

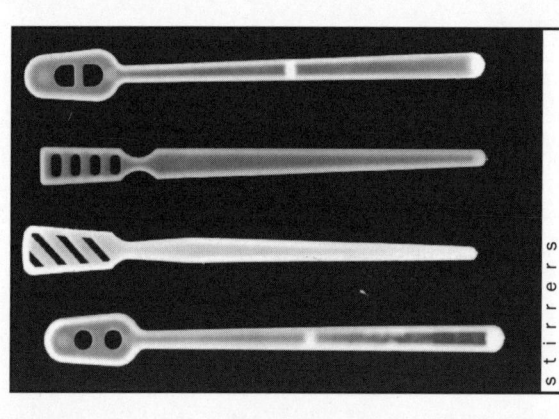
stirrers

way I first heard it. The guy telling it ended by chanting Jimmy's mantra with two fingers pinched on the end of his nose (I'b god doe job, doe fabbily, doe dose...). I heard the story in a pub while I was still trying to find my feet and finding them too fast for my liking. I guess it's true that you can take a boy out of the town but can't take the town of the boy. I laughed at the story but left the pub with a down home feeling. I was home and I was down.

Over the next week, I went out drinking most days and nights and heard the story another four times. The last time from Jimmy No-Nose himself. He was forty seven and would have been balding if he wasn't already bald. The burn skin covered his head like melted plastic, held in place by fake ears that could have been taken from Mr Potato Head. His eyes were blue and completely round, they were held into their sockets by taut, almost clear, skin. He had no nose and his nostrils were two tear drops above a soft moustache of wispy hair transplanted from some place else.

Jimmy spoke with a soft, hiccuping voice. He had only a slight impediment and a beautiful accent of a type that's begun to disappear. It was the voice of an older uncle, a tradesman, a mechanic. I enjoyed listening to him. Every word he spoke was an invitation to joke. He had his one-liners and he had his simple philosophy: he was the luckiest man in the world. At any rate, there

gun

were plenty of buggers a sight worse off. I liked him and when we'd finished our drinks I stood on the pavement and waited to share my cab with him.

He asked me inside for a nightcap. He meant it, he knew I wasn't a user but he said he had a drop of whiskey indoors. I could drink that, he'd do a bit of the other. I said, 'Sure.'

Sat above him, on the arm of his sofa, I said, 'There's something odd about your story. Four of your mates pick you up at the hospital and invite you for a celebration? You're a good lad, Jimmy, but junkies aren't usually so generous.'

'I gob good mates, me.'

I said, 'Yeah, you've got mates. When you've got a bag of shit stashed at home, stuff that you'd only tried once and now was just sitting waiting until you were well enough to leave the hospital, then you've got mates.'

'No. You'b gob ib wrong, son.'

I hadn't though. He'd set himself up as a wholesaler and he'd blown it. No matter how you feel personally, fools and amateurs can't just run around doing things their own sweet way. No professional would ever sell ninety per cent pure smack, they don't want their customers dying on them. The people I work for sell safe gear. They reach understandings with other professionals. The shite, like Jimmy No-Nose, they pay me to get rid of. Amateurs do nothing but bring down the price, bring down the police and end up killing people.

author

Jimmy was lucky all right. He was lucky his habit was so old that he hadn't overdosed the day he was working on his car, hours before he set himself on fire. But he'd just run out of luck.

Nicholas Blincoe is the author of *Acid Casuals* and *Jello Salad*.

Carol Swain is working on a 2nd graphic novel. Her 1st, *Invasion of the Mind Sappers*, was published by Fantagraphics.

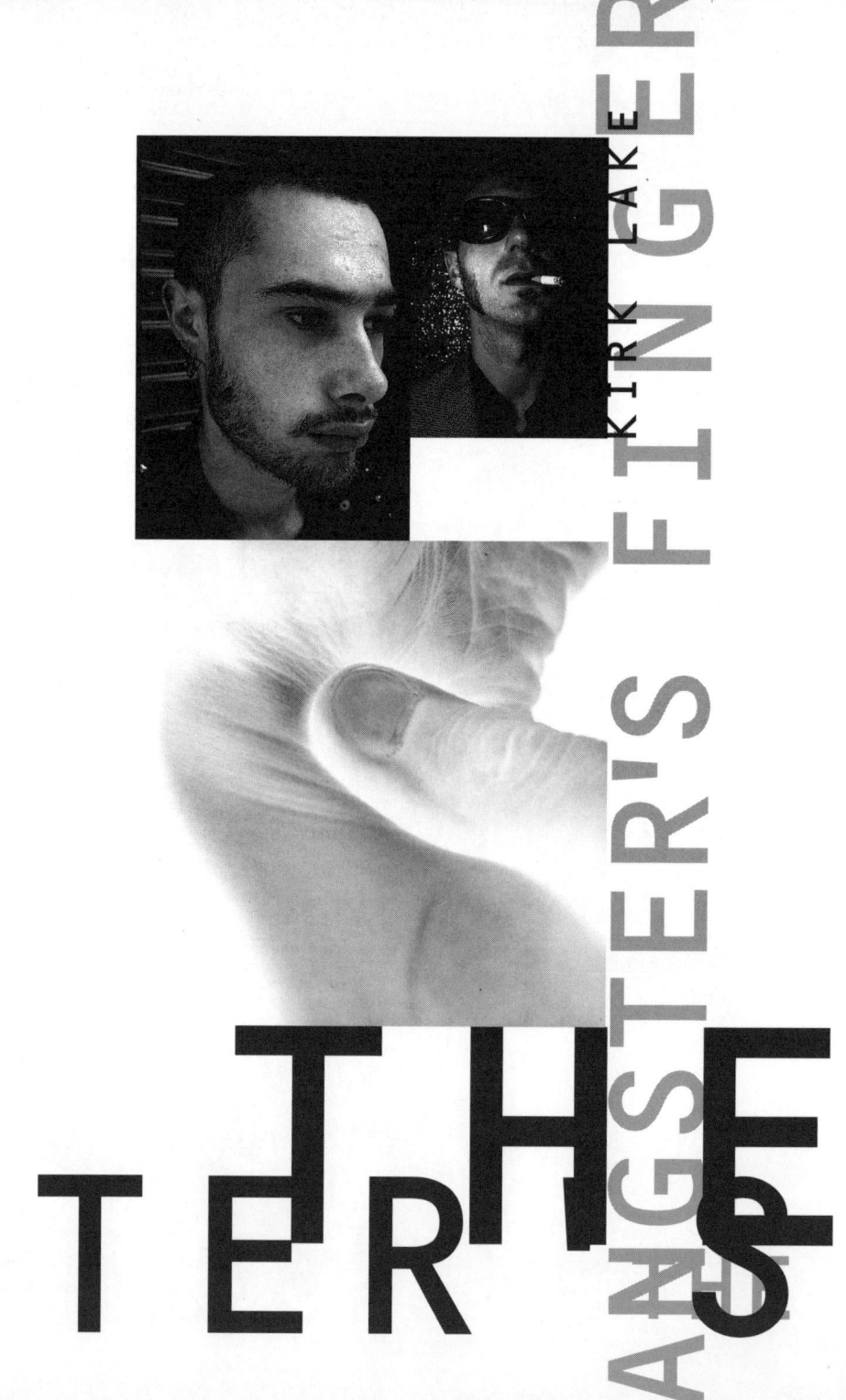

...you know it was like that time the Bug lost some of his teeth to Steward. He was in on this long pool session, playing through the night in a room above a sandwich bar on Cricklewood Broadway. He'd been up for a while but Steward must've hustled him good because by the time dawn was coming on he'd already lost all of his money, had IOUs stacked on top of IOUs and Steward had even filched his fucking wedding ring man. Wouldn't fit on anything but his little finger but he'd flaunt it at the Bug like this, tapping his finger every time he bridged. So the Bug had nothing left to play with and he started putting on his jacket and getting out of there when Steward offered him one more frame saying that he'd give the Bug a chance to win back all of his money. So the Bug says yeah, but what have I got to bet with, you've got the fucking lot already and Steward says I'll play you for your gold tooth, all the money I won against that tooth. You saw the tooth right? Yeah, course that's why we called him the Bug, after Bugs Bunny, that stupid too big gold tooth he had sticking out the top of his jaw. Well this was a bad night turning into a bad morning for the Bug and when he got five-balled in that last frame he tried to make a run for the door but Steward just swung the butt of that black cue-stick of his right into the Bug's face and the gold tooth, and pretty damn near every other one of his teeth came popping out onto the carpet. Ha, yeah I know it. But I guess the Bug'll always be called the Bug even without that gold tooth. Y'know, Steward had it drilled and has it dangling from his key chain. Funny bastard that Steward, really funny...

I didn't answer. I looked up at Perry. I saw his lips moving.

GANGSTER FINGER NIGGER

I saw his face crack and a little dribble of spit run down the corner of his mouth when he laughed. I watched his bandaged hands weaving around in front of my face as he acted out his story. I even wondered for one split second how long the ash on the cigarette he held but didn't smoke would grow before it dropped off on to the kitchen tiles.
I looked up at Perry. But I wasn't listening to anything he said.

On the table was a saucerful of glitter and sequins. Next to this was a cardboard crown covered in silver foil with glitter stripes running along the bottom of it and crusts of sequins glued on at each point. **THE KING** was written in black marker across the foil in scratchy uneven letters with the N written backwards as if it was in a mirror. It was the saddest thing I can ever remember seeing. Not because it was badly made. Not because it looked as if it would fall apart if I picked it up. But because it had been made with such hope. Such tongue-out-the-corner-of-the-mouth concentration. Perry's kid with his glue stick and his scissors. Perry's kid now fast asleep in the bedroom next door. Sweet dreams. And Perry and me sat around the kitchen table, watching the clock, waiting for the as yet undecided moment to go out and commit an act of such desperate lunacy, that even I had difficulty in coming up with one single good reason not to carry it through. An act of such monumental idiocy that it went beyond reason.

Perry had started talking about kidnapping three months previously. I'd played along because it was something to talk about. We sat in the pub and discussed who or what would be a good target. Perry was set on taking the Koi carp out of the ornamental pool in the park and then driving them down south and selling them on. I pointed out that, in fact, that wasn't kidnapping at all. That was just stealing. Though it did seem to me to be a possibility and one that I suggested we kept in mind. I favoured kidnapping a dog. We could probably pick up a grand or so with very little risk if we targetted the right animal.

We set about trying to locate a likely looking victim and a likely looking pet. We loitered around the park and the recreation grounds.

We parked outside the vet's and sat watching from Perry's car for a couple of afternoons. We drew up a list of three candidates. Three dogs that we had followed home from their walks right up to the drive-ways of their affluent looking detached homes. And we finally decided to go after a spaniel called Kent that lived in a house with a Range Rover and a Jaguar parked outside and a burglar alarm and security lights above the doorway. *They must have stuff in there that's worth stealing,* Perry had said. *They must have money to pay a ransom.*

The owner took the dog out three times a day. Once at 7:30am and then later at 6pm and then finally at 11pm. We had watched this every day for a week. We were thorough in our research. The early evening walk offered the best opportunity for a snatch. The owner, a middle-aged man with greying hair and a slight stoop, walked the dog to the recreation ground and then let him off his lead while he sat on a bench and read a book. He was either a very slow reader or he just had the book for something to hold in his hands. We saw him every night for a week and it was always the same Eric Ambler novel and he never got past the first few pages.

A few minutes before six and we were hiding in the bushes beside the chain fence that separated the car park from the recreation ground. Perry's car was parked behind us with the engine running. He'd cleared the boot and put a rug down inside it in case the dog got sick or crapped while we were driving it away. In his hand he held a stinking bone. Scraps of flesh had turned green and flies were landing on it and buzzing around us. I had a hessian sack rolled up under my arm. We peered out towards the bench. Just after six the man came, let the dog off the lead, sat on the bench and opened his book. The dog came running right by us.

Kent...Kent... Perry hissed and waved the bone. I got ready with the sack. *Kent... Here boy... here boy...* The dog came over to us. Perry reached out with the bone. *Get ready with the sack. We're gonna get the little fucker.* The dog came nearer. I had the sack open. I moved out from behind Perry and got ready to jump. Maybe I frightened it. I don't know. That's what Perry said. *You stupid fucking bastard you could've got me killed.* Slowly, I said, slllloooooowwwwlllly... *not jump out and wave the sack like a fucking flag.*

(43)

Next thing the dog is growling and snapping and has his teeth embedded in Perry's right hand and then as Perry's trying to beat him off with the stinking bone he gets his teeth embedded in his left hand. And the dog's barking and Perry's yelping and I'm stood staring at the owner who's come over to see what's going on and is calling off his dog and calling us a couple of perverts for hanging out in bushes and I'm trying to hide the sack and I'm grabbing Perry and pushing him through the gap in the chain fence and into his car and driving him to casualty to get a tetanus shot.

    We gave up on the dogs.

    Then we were sat in the pub watching the television news a week or so after Operation Kent had disintegrated. A story came on about the funeral of a top gangster. Film of the procession. The coffin in a glass carriage drawn by horses. Streets lined with people like it was the Silver Jubilee or something. Film at the church. Weeping celebrities. Weeping family. The coffin being carried into the churchyard by pall-bearers that looked like the toughest, meanest bouncers you'd ever seen. We had actually decided that maybe kidnapping wasn't for us. We'd just been talking about it right before the news had come on. We watched the funeral. I looked at Perry. Perry looked at me. *Yes!* we said. *Yes!* We said it at exactly the same instant.

I dipped my hand into the saucer. Pressed my fingers into the glitter. Drank from a cold mug of tea. Looked out the window. It was beginning to get lighter. We had the radio on. An old red vinyl Roberts tuned into the oldies station. Billy Fury was singing 'Maybe Tomorrow'. I looked at the clock.

    —We should go if we're going.

    I made a move to get up from the chair but ended up just sitting back down. Perry was tightening the bandages on his hands. Pulling on them with his teeth and attempting to secure a safety pin into the yellowing fabric.

    —Yeah. I guess we should. If we leave it much longer it'll be too light and we'll be seen.

    —One thing though Perry. How are we going to prove that we've actually got him. I mean as soon as the story breaks there's going to be a dozen people calling up saying, *It's me. I've got him. I want some money.*

—We'll cut off his little finger.

—What?

—We'll cut off a fucking finger.

—Why?

—So we can send it to them. Then they'll know we've really got him.

—I don't know. That's a little sick isn't it?

—What are you saying man? We're sitting here getting ready to go and dig up a dead body. Fuck.

—Yeah, yeah okay. Say we do cut it off. How's that going to prove anything... it could be anybody's finger.

—Think about it. The guy is, I mean was, one of the most famous gangsters this country's ever known. His prints will be on file.

Perry got up from the table and took his coat from the peg behind the door.

—Okay let's go. I'll meet you in the car. I'm going to get the spades from the garden.

I watched him walk out the back door. I looked at my hands and my fingertips glittered. I reached over and picked up the crown and placed it on my head and looked at my reflection in the kitchen window. *I am the King.* On the radio Billy Fury was still singing. I leaned over and turned him off.

Kirk Lake has released 2 albums of "low-life yarns and thug jazz". The most recent is the *5 finger discount* EP on I Records. He lives in London. His novel *Never Hit the Ground* is due to be published later this year.

A BAD NIGHT LIFE IN ONE SHORT PART

TIM ETCHELLS

German Fukker

When great chart fame and fortune came to the talentless crooner Fokker in his 25th yr, his whole life took on that dire air and weight of bad pop video, all things done cheap and surreal. Living in Manchester, Endland (sic) his girls were anorexic would-be sphinxes, his house was full of pigeons, doves or waterfalls and each nite before he slept mixed-race blokes in silver jump-suit type outfits would mouth glistening incomprehensible words on top of a brite green hill near his housing estate.

   Of course the bastard council sent people round, complaints abt noise and animal treatment, and a poxy lawsuit followed with some fans what had written Fokker's name and album title on the pavement outside his door. Managers and agents hassled Fokker, calling him up all time when he just wanted to sleep and go down in slow motion with his mates.

   If all that crap were 'the price of fame' © Fokker was soon bored—a lifetime's ambition burned up in weeks nearly—the stupid turd growing old before his time, not really liking life. So what if his 'new record' was number three (3) in a chart or if some big lawyer and quantity control bloke from Mexico wanted to see him. On a typical day he (a) could not get his tv to sit straight on the lilo, (b) got a leak in his waterbed and (c) spent all nite riding thru rain in some dickhead car looking for a big rave in a field what turned out to be cancelled.

One night at his house and at the height of his boredom and fame an angel come to Fokker in a dream and told him he had to go to LAZARUS, a club in Rotherham where a bloke had died and then come back. Lazarus was a DJ now it seemed and played slow beats slower than the devil himself.

Guest list, stretch pants and shirt by Stephen Berkoff, Fokker got a black cab to LAZARUS where he got out of the door (of the cab) and put each of his feet on the pavement, one by one, lifting them and then putting them down repeatedly and thus moving forwards until he got to the door. Sometimes it seemed now that even the simplest things were difficult for Fokker.

Kids in the club recognised Fokker but were too cool to say owt, whispering the name of his band and latest crap-concept album. In centre of the room a gang of 1st Div footballers in elaborate glam drag were dancing round a pile of handbags belonging to their wives or girlfriends. This were a strange scene indeed, made stranger by the lighting all of a puke greenish hue. At edges of the room were more dancers on scaffolding and a booth where the DJs were. Inside that booth which was mentioned before an old looking Japanese bloke was talking over the music (never a good thing in a DJ), and describing at some length his experiences on August 13th 1945 in Hiroshima — the way the bomb blast had shook him and the way his skin had seemed for a moment to be of translucent colour and how he had even seen rite thru his bones. Of all this talking no one batted an eyelid at it but Fokker couldn't quite get hip to the beat — maybe the Jap rapper was all part of the LAZARUS idea he thought — other blokes who'd nearly died doing PA's in the club or something, the odd allnighter in a mortuary, Fokker didn't know anyhow, and, being German, had no sense of humour whatsoever about anything.

After a long time the Jap bloke stopped talking and the slow beat theme carried on with a less than catchy tune sounding like a mixture of late Kray Twins and early Hawker Siddley. Footballers left the dancefloor in a hurry and it soon thronged full with daft twats showing off to straight girls waiting to get married and play housey housey.

Fokker nodded to some people he thought he probably knew but didn't and bought a packet of fags from a machine in the corner by the bogs, getting strange looks from a group of kids what were lurking in its shadow and who until recently had had their heads buried in polythene bags full of glue. Fokker was exactly that sort of bloke what slept in the daytime and went out in the 'nightime' © but even he had to admit 'true cause' that the niteclub LAZARUS was weird:
— A tv in the corner showed a boxing match with Joe DiMaggio.
— A poster on the wall was for a new boy-band called FAECES.
— Two ex-miners were stood at the bar discussing the ill-fortune of their various video shops, opened on redundancy cash in 85 and now getting driven into crisis by Blockbuster/Ritz.

A kid on the other side of the cavernous hall caught Fokker's eye and beckoned him over. It was all like that bit on the advert for Cadbury's Chocolate Nooses ® where the tank is rolling past a city skyline in flames, and them soldiers on the gibbet exchange a look of love and laughter and hatred and brotherhood and struggle and passion and hope and understanding and forgiveness and violence and more love and wisdom and guilt and pride for just a few seconds before the trapdoor opens and they fall.

The kid gestured to a chair and bade Fokker sit down, a smile right on his mouth. Hi sed Fokker, hi sed the kid and Fokker palmed a little bottle of drugs the kid handed him and, after 'sundry chit chat' and 'mouthing off for no reason' © he slipped off to the loo. In the bogs a black girl from New York was selling hairspray, condoms, combs and other crap, all laid out on a makeshift cardboard-box table. A bloke was pissing in the urinal and talking to his mate but, since looking down at his dick in strange concentration, now totally unaware that his mate had long gone:

"Yeah," he was saying as Fokker stumbled out of his cubicle, the drug starting to work in him already. "Marion and I hev sold de house and are goin up country for an little while. I want to live right out of there man, I mean right out there, where de air is clean you know and de Insomnia is pure..."

Fokker only read the label on the bottle (of drugs) after he had taken it all which is not really the most sensible way to do it but it works for some people. HEROINE it said on the bottle (when he did bother to read it) and indeed it wasn't long before one arrived— a skinny girl in a very short pastel skirt, a black and white top and a thin gold chain glinting round her tanned exposed midriff. Hi sed Fokker and she sed hi back proving at least that conversation was not yet dead in the country of Endland (sic). Her name, it transpired, was Miranda.

Lowered from the ceiling on his bed Lazarus entered the DJ booth in flamboyant style and started his second set. There was the sound of choppers in the air outside the club or tent or whatever and rumours that police (the pigs) were arresting the whole queue of people outside. Everyone inside didn't seem to mind. Lazarus put a record or two on—one by Abba and the other by Slade but he couldn't seem to get people dancing. He put on more tunes—by Heater and by Nobody and by Rolf Harris and so on—so soon there was five (5) songs all playing at the same time. Fokker was more a singer/crooner than a back-from-the-dead DJ type but even he could see that Lazarus was good, if a little clumsy on the turntable and unorthodox in his methods.

When folks did get moving you couldn't exactly tell if maybe it was for Coldstream Guards or The Belsen or Smokey but anyway when they did get moving it were like L could do no wrong etc playing the crowd like it were a music instrument of which he had the absolute master race blah blah. Fokker kept watching, his eyes 'wide'. Just when it looked like 'quite a good do' tho, Lazarus cut the mood and went into a long long slow rap about life before death and life after death and other crap, clearing the floor. Only Miranda in the whole club and the whole world danced to this Lazarus rap — snaking and turning slowly in the middle of the dancefloor all alone while Fokker watched her from the rail and a crowd of black blokes made a circle round her and wolf whistling, clapping their hands and nodding wisely at the good dancing.

It was sometime in Miranda's dance that Fokker started to feel a bit funny and strange like the HEROINE was really pretty strong, maybe cut with something, maybe not. He had the impression (like the poets say) that he was drunk and 'sinking and rising at the same time' © and later he saw a vague hallucination of a zebra up amongst party decorations in the club roof. When he checked his watch (a really good one which seemed to have a M. Mouse face and everything) he found it had slowed and then, only moments later, stopped. The slow beats were indeed running very slow that nite, Lazarus well into his groove and all kids in the club creeping about like their very feet were the royalty of whispering.

Fokker watched Miranda dance, her hands pulling colours from the air but when he felt too weird he looked round vaguely for the bloke what sold him the HEROINE to ask him (1) what the fuck it was and (2) how long it lasted and (3) if there were probably any dangerous side effects etc, but he couldn't see him. Too late. Even the footballers seemed wild and otherworldly now, just barely recognisable behind the large pyramid of beer glasses they had built, Bobby Moore and Arthur Ramsey laughing uproariously at David Platt who was sinking a third pint while a fourth (4th) one was balanced on his head.

Miranda danced — flat stomach, her arms snakes, eyes black of nothing, slow beats so slow that when Fokker checked his pulse, leaned against a pillar he could not find it at all, dark closing in at the edges of his vision.

For one moment he thought he saw the lights of the club swim, shift and combine to tell him a message, moving slowly into focus with Miranda in the centre but then Lazarus changed his groove again and the beats slowed even more, some track by Freud about the uncanny, with a riff on heimlich/unheimlich, heimlich/unheimlich, a chill of ice in the air and Fokker went falling to the floor in so very many pieces.

Three weeks later F woke up in a hospital going cold turkey from HEROINE. The girl missing and despite all enquires like no one knew her, no one saw her and no one even registered her name. Of the bloke what dealt him the drug no sign neither. Fokker wept on tabloid tv, did interviews from intensive care and like OJ Simpson promising to catch the real killer of Nicole Brown he promised that he too (once better) would scour the real world only looking for Miranda.

Fokker needn't have bothered though. One nite while he was sleeping on the ward she came back to him, in costume of a nurse and she danced for him again and while she danced he glimpsed his heartbeat on the EEG, the spikes and beats of it slowing, rippling, slowing, like real slow beats, lime green spikes on dark green ground, Miranda dancing and Fokker saw the lines on the EEG go crazy for a moment, spike beat, skip beat and then ripple and then turn into birds, the birds flying over the screen, lime green birds on dark green ground, wings beating slowly slowly and then gone.

FOKKER DEAD ran the headlines next day.
    GIRL MISSING.
    ENDLAND DREAMING.
Fokker's album went double platinum and his manager got rich.

Tim Etchells is a writer and director best known for his work with the award winning Sheffield-based outfit *Forced Entertainment* who were recently hailed by *The Guardian* as "Britain's most brilliant experimental theatre company". His novel *Helen* © is a huge and bitter monster in 3rd-draft stage.

west

Friday soho drunken binge is used to collect amusing foreigners. Mexican in Oxford Street attempts to burn a twenty pound note because you won't take it from him. Basques waft amyl nitrate in your face, Sufis convert you. A Saturday morning is a time to compare your collection with your friends.

Saturday night the experience is repeated, this time maybe Brixton. Here the aim is gangsters, encounters with interesting tramps will not do. In a club you slide down with your back against the wall and comment on people's legs. Markets are the place for picking up real bargains. Camden is both inexpensive and fun, very crowded so don't be misanthropic. Danger of meeting goths in the Electric Ballroom.

emma payne

Conversations must start more ambitiously than *what's your name*. No one knows the secret, pluck it from out of the air to fit the occasion. Loud laughter will signal success or humiliating failure.

Hanway Street is for late night drinking. The landlady's name is Helen. The chat is of creative projects: rub your face against the velvet curtains and feel the Fifties slip through your fingers. A shower of fag ash leaves you in a drift. The stairs to the toilet are for sliding down, to make a long painful graze for later.

You are at the only occupied table in an empty establishment. To find where they've all gone, check Time Out for details, or walk down Greek Street calling and peering into darkened windows. A fashionably dressed man standing on the corner won't tell you, even if he knows.

The cab firms add your name to their list but your number never comes up. Start walking and you'll regret it; streets all look the same in the dark. Kneel on the pavement and sob into the gutter. This will get you nowhere, fast.

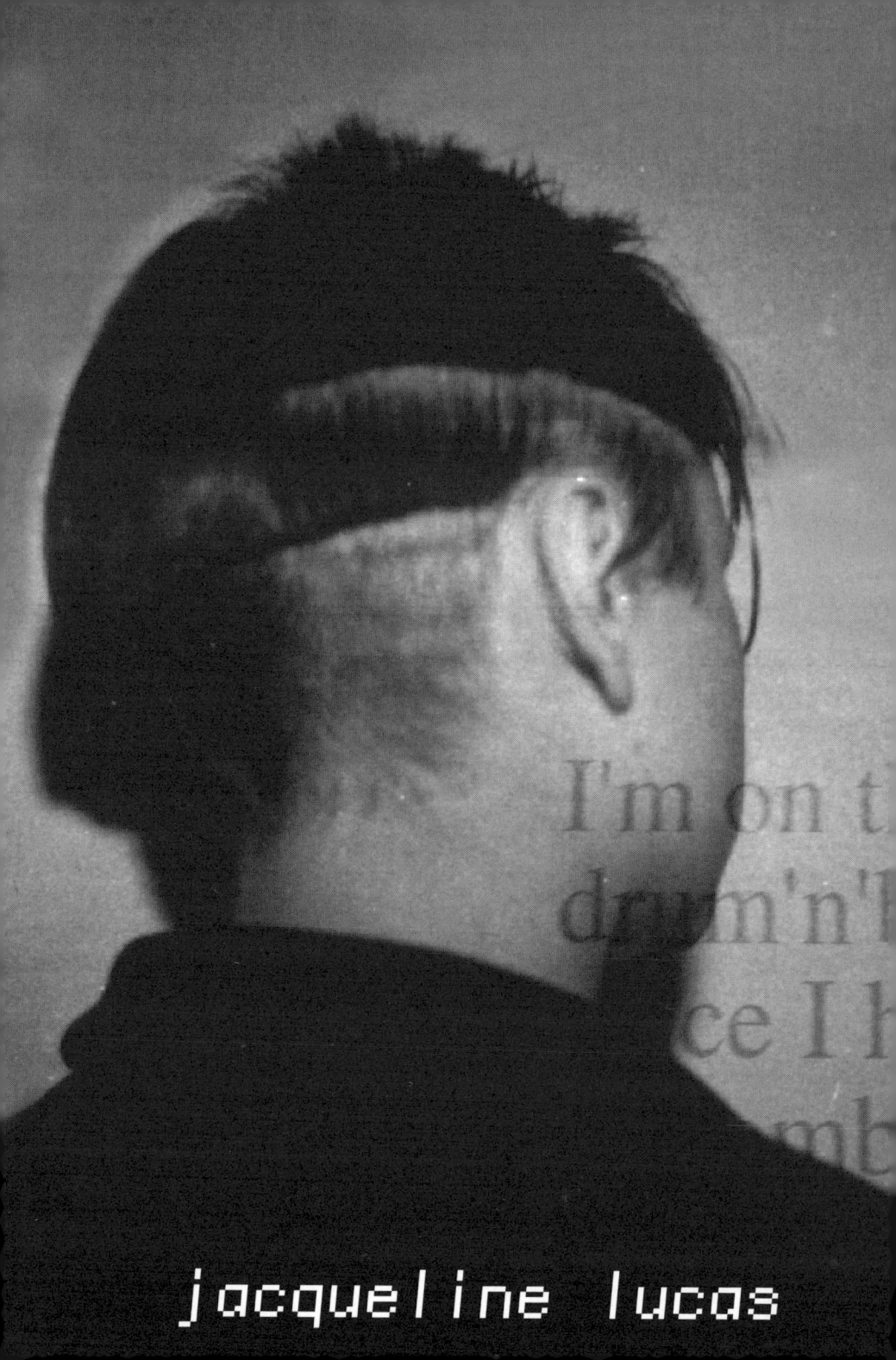

I'm on the floor to the tunes of asian jazzy jungly drum'n'bass and maybe it's because it's ages since I had a good dance and maybe 'cause I remember sundays when freestyle jazz dancers took to the floor and the floor's mine and I'm heading round it in crazy moves I feel inside as I jerk and rock my head from side to side make Indian circles with my hand belly dance arabian stylee then pogue into the air like a teenager at PT. It's like my soul's bursting out my shell and I don't care what I look like 'cause this feels so good and I'm laughing and I know it looks like I'm off my face and I'm off my face but it's all in the music.

outcaste

You look like a real raver, this gorgeous asian girl says and I think you're fucking right there and I suddenly wish it was him on the dancefloor that said that. The him with cream harem pants and matching knee length tunic who looks like the cover of my Nitin Sawhney album which is why me and my mate are here. Nitin takes me to heaven but he doesn't look like the picture on the album I fell in love with before I came.

This is the man I've come here for tonight and he's half my age and dark dark dark black eyes and he's moving on the floor as if he knows inside and it takes forever as I edge my way towards all the while an eye on the girls around him, little girls who can't touch us as we catch each other's eye from one tune to the next admiring the other's body tuned to the soundbites like they're rising through our chests as we follow with the moves the music makes us.

I'm so amazed entertained at discovering my body's will I feel like I've arrived my spirit's found a home and I can see this man in my peripheral vision no matter where my elaborate twists and jerks and jumps and swirling madness take me always checking out what he's up to. Him with the face that says I don't need anyone I'm young the girls love me the boys love me they come to me they always come to me as he skips and bobs on his little demarcated space of the floor.

Do these nights happen every week? I cry in the ear of another asian babe who thinks I'm on the make as she strains to tell me it's an Outcaste thing and I mumble pseudo-perception. Tonight I'm the outcast waiting for the asian DJ who pretends she'll get to me but continues to mix and push her buttons without so much as a nod. And I head back to the floor 'cause I'm never going to charm her into a sample tape not even a name to search in world music at HMV.

I'm sweating like fuck now and I'm glad I don't know what I look like 'cause I'm back to my sampling of world dance styles that I explore as if in the privacy of my own bedroom to no one but me. Tonight I share my secret moves and my friend Steffi laughs back at me often as she sees my demented turns. I keep my distance 'cause I know I'm half incredible and half embarrassing and she's never seen me in my element like this sharing my hips and belly with the dancefloor being twelve and forty at the same time.

 Dark Eyes and I register each other and I feel like a stalker circling my prey 'cause he stays in his demarcated girly section to the left of the stage and I pogue and hop and gyrate my way edging as if imperceptibly closer but like I don't know 'cause I'm turning and shouting into the ears of people around me what's this track? as they respond or raise their eyebrows as if it doesn't matter as if they've got all the time in the week in week out to return to Dingwalls or the Blue Note or wherever DJ Rathu is expressing herself on our account.

 I feel half stupid 'cause I'm pretending I'm not next to him now and turning my back and moving as if far away and not exchanging glances like we were from a distance. The two main ravers of the dancefloor didn't she tell me that and he's the other one and I can feel Steffi laughing at me as I make my slow all evening beeline to this moment to this beautiful boy till I'm facing him now and I'm a magnet for his moves having lost all desire to whirl and gyrate in my own hemisphere. Like a mirror I don't surprise connecting every move he makes without so much as a word or a nod or eyeball just here I am as I jump in his wake to the left to the right with our arms then our feet then our heads which we shake at each other and soon we're smiling as we do things to each other on the floor as he throws his fists towards me and I jump back in play returning the punches at him to the jungly beats as he reels from me and returns my throws. We're in complete head with the sounds and each other as I shoot my legs out in kicks towards him my torso leaning back away and we switch as I lean into his body as he kicks me away and

I want to sweep him up in my sweaty arms and carry him home laughing but we can't keep this up I'm out of breath and out of shape and pretending I'm with the powerfully young hormones jumping around me but I have to switch as if naturally into my araby belly or my ecstasy arms to cool it and save myself from collapse.

He is doing the same as he switches from the hysteria of our jungle beats to the keyboards for his next directive. He's into hopping and skipping like a scottish dance we did at school and I'm back in step without a glance of recognition just here I am again crossing my feet and jumping side to side as I mirror his footwork and direction while my body cries out to scottish dance him to the door load him in my car and my face says this is nothing this is fun I'm an old hand at dancing and you're good so I like it but this means nothing and my friend Steffi in the corner who I belly dance towards at longer and longer intervals is maybe the woman I'm with and you know nothing about me and I'll be off soon so take this as nothing but my desires of the spirit as I connect your every move my body always ending up here in just this little part of the floor and no other as I head towards you slowly to marry my footsteps with yours.

We're enjoying this creating more and more loony gestures and there's two of us now looking good as we follow each other's deranged motions the arms crossing each other staccato the heads jerking in berserk fits like gunshot like a speeded up dog on a car dash I feel for days maybe weeks.

He's branched into his own moves or was it me it's hard to pinpoint as I watch another girl approach him. This one's asian with frizzy black curls and maybe twenty and he's cool as ever and I wonder is he married? A strict hindu with child bride who's here with the Outcaste brigade. Suddenly exhausted I take my sweaty body back to my friend who's almost ready to call it a night as I lie down theatrically on a row of chairs and opt out to take up observation. I am giving up the fight. The fight that says I can look as good as you I am young and trendy in my swirly pop art Wanton Diesel dress and my secondhand nylon gym trousers with stripes up the side and my Nike trainers which are sweating inside and out with my knackered bare feet and my dyed black at the roots hair and the dancefloor is emptying and Nitin and co are on stage dismantling their gear and Steffi tells me one last go? and I attack the floor with a final attempt to break through to Dark Eyes have him tell me his name, lean over towards me mid jungly saying can I go with you somewhere after the club 'cause I've loved our dancing and I feel we're kindred spirits and to be honest I find you terribly attractive but I'm rather shy and not terribly good at this and please don't be offended if you're here with your girlfriend, is she your girlfriend? And I lean in close and whisper, no. I've just loved dancing with you and I haven't done it in ages and I want to do it again and I also find you frighteningly attractive maybe it's a mirror thing you know you dance like me and look like me or something and yes please let's just hurry out of here and not even stop to say our goodbyes.

    But it's harder to do 'cause the dancefloor is sparse and the lights coming up and my beeline to join him a lot more upfront and my age more material in the house lights even though I've refreshed my purple Mac lipstick and the insides of my mouth with a sugarless Cloret and I'm thrilled to see a boy with darker hair in a sixties Oasis cut and italian gear grinning eagerly at me which takes the edge of my middle aged bid towards Black Eyes as I edge towards him for my final session on the floor. A last scottish hop skip and jump destined for him as I summon the last trace of teenage memory to transcend my body and RAVE RAVE RAVE.

    The lights come up the volume down as I address him. The boy who's consumed my momentum all night and I'll be blowed if I leave without so much as goodbye. Jac, I offer. Confirming my borderline sexuality as I plant my handshake like a bank manager all jolly. Ikbar, he says. Ikbar, I try out hoping for something. I've enjoyed dancing with you, he says as if to a teacher who's helped him with the placement of his decimal point. I ask him what I know already. Is this a weekly event? Till we follow politely the Outcaste story and I introduce Steffi. Ikbar, Steffi. I hope to see you again, I say as if my toes would like another go at an asian drum'n'bass boogie. Yes, he says. I leave with her, stand alone while she undoes her bike inviting Dark Eyes who I imagine circling the space behind me.

    Hey! Let's swap! Where did you get that top? It's amazing! he tells me and I recognise my italian. Bobby, he holds out his hand grinning. Diesel, I tell him, it's easy. And he takes me through his wardrobe. Only fifteen quid from Mr Byrite, he thrills. Where are you from? I ask, hoping to burst into mediterranean soundbites as I notice the mark on his forehead the murmur in the group outside. Where do you think planet Mars? says an asian babe, as I swallow my decades long hungarian russian jewish englishness, the where-are-you-fromness I notice no longer. Italian. Didn't you say something to me in italian on the floor? Oh, *I'm* sorry. We share a last word on style as he asks how to tell me about the next gig. Jac. I'm on the Outcaste list, I tell him.

    I walk Steffi's bike to the corner and half turn my white face to watch the remaining group converge round a motor car as I walk slowly into the early morning light of Camden Town. My movements no longer in tandem with Ikbar's. My arms and feet free to fall in step with Chalk Farm Road and the pace of the night. Can you give us a fag? I hand a man my last of ten. Give us a lift into Camden Palace? he partly jokes as I swing my two-seater north towards Hampstead and sleep.

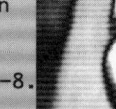

Jacqueline Lucas has had stories published in *A Be Sea*, *Ambit* & *Em*. She is a poet and photographer concentrating on getting up the duff and recording the awkward moments on Hi-8.

SUNDAY night

Super powers on

How can that cunt be late again, it's just not possible. Missy is talking to herself outside Great Portland Street station and not best pleased. She doesn't realise that I'm fighting with my sister and her friends to sell the last few pills I've got left at a reasonable price — one that won't let me lose face. Being girls of fifteen who think they know it all they're giving it plenty and trying the comedy rate. We're not up North now for God's sake, I say. My figure is much higher.

But Missy isn't to know this. She has no room in her life for diversions or complications. Instead she calls Helen on her creaky old mobile with a case that's a size too big and bad-mouths me for a good half hour on my no-show. We're supposed to be checking out the Albany crew for a Sunday night pre-op session. Why is he doing this? she asks Helen, her head tucked into the temperamental German machine as if it might just do something for a change, like give her an answer. Fuck Niven, says Hels through the crackle. Come down to work, I've got an hour free, come now.

Missy cabs it down to the Sports Cafe where Hels works the bar. Being summer it is choc full of weary Northern and foreign families, hen-night girl gangs and predatory beer boys, all stuffing down the complimentary bar snacks like there's no tomorrow and spending mucho money on drink in order to keep the wretched things down. She knocks on the staff door and finds Hels roaching a spliff atop a Euro 96 souvenir brochure. Right on cue, grins Hels, thrilled because she thought her Sunday night was going to be a non-starter. Take this. She hands over the trumpet-sized cheeba, moving to her locker to magic a catering size bottle of Gordon's. Let's get started, and after this it's into the jungle.

So much for our date. I'm on a street corner somewhere near the flyover, buzzing on the rocket fuel I scored from James's neighbour this afternoon. It's good stuff. My nails are cut to the quick, red raw, they blunt through the buzz. I run the tips gently along the pavement to accentuate it. I am moving out of skatewear into this year's autumn/winter: today it's a grey half suit from Helmut Lang with a top that started its life in New York. Everyone has complimented me on it. It's good enough to show Missy, though I'm not really in the mood to turn up there now. She can smoke herself to infinity in the Sports Cafe for all I care. (You see, I know everything.) It's much more fun hanging here with my sisters. Thanks to them I'm sixty quid richer. I'm smoking their fags (Embassy) to show them my gratitude. Come out with us, says Twigs. It'll only be Bag Lady's or somewhere like that, but it'll be a laugh. Yeah come on, chips in one of the hyenas. To a rave in Helmut Lang, I'm thinking, you've got to be joking. But I've already shovelled a pill down my throat to complement everything I've had so far, so I say, Fine, cool. Let's trip.

Bag Lady's is inexplicably shut so we find ourselves in the darkest of lockups a couple of blocks down, immediately caught in a sea of bomber jackets and the like the moment we enter. Fighting for the perfect space somewhere in the centre of the floor, the entire area rammed with kids who have no intention of going to their modular science double tomorrow morning — they're getting all the chemistry they need tonight. Why isn't there a GCSE in trance induction or something, a BTEC in Class A? The pass rate would be phenomenal.

Tonight I'm passing in and out of myself, dancing like a possessed something I haven't seen for a while. My girls are equally shaman-like, not caring who they pull or what fucking record follows the next, so long as it stays hard and above 130 bpm. We're lit by phosfluorescents and strobes alternately, which cut through my shirt creating a mini Soudeni-inspired laser explosion. Tina and co would kill for that kind of effect and it's all happening quite naturally right here. When the ultraviolet flickers momentarily to greet us I catch sight of a hyena's nipple ring hiding behind a thick white vest from Calvin Klein. I'm still moving with the beats, but the moment of the glance itself seems to last as long as the night. Checking the kids out from time to time on the floor, it appears that everyone is as fucked as we are and enjoying it immensely. It's probably three o'clock now (how?) but there's no question of going home just yet. I share water with Twiglet and the hyenas at their insistence and realise I haven't had a lager for at least three hours and feel great because of it. Beer muddies things. The pill, and it's a strong one, overtakes the effect of the evening's lines so I'm chatting a lot less but thinking LONGERHARDERFASTERMORE. I was never one for waving my hands in the air but for once the mood overtakes me and I'm unselfconsciously facing upward greeting the light. It is warm yet blinding, an overwhelming white blindness I long to consume me. Wanky but true. It's the only way I can account for these last few hours — the need to be where the light is, having acquired the fastest of heartbeats to run with it.

Over at Adrenalin Village, Missy and Helen are also playing homage to the free spirit. Compelled by the high boy:girl ratio that the club attracts they dance, stoned, crossing the breakbeats and forgetting that I even exist.

Govinden, 23, lives for: pProgressiveUKHouse, fast cars, Bond, Soul records that are EEP, Dolce e Gabbana, Lucky e, Masters at Work, Drum & Bass, on Network, Hip Hop that cuts, Baduizm.

67

What I was really into then was seventies music. Well, it was the decade I was born in. My favourites were Chic and Rolls Royce and sometimes if I was feeling really high it would be Sister Sledge or the Doobie Brothers. But my record collection was not just classics-only territory, oh no. I listened to anything that lifted me. I hated all that techno stuff that was around last year. Last year you were into techno or seventies. That's how it was.

My girlfriend at the time was Sherree; or that's what I called her. Her name was really Cheryl, but I preferred Sherree. She always took so long to get ready. "Come on baby," I'd call. "I'll be right there Dave," she would say, and then she would be another half an hour applying her lipstick or whatever she did in the bathroom that took so long. And I would look at my watch every few minutes, thinking every few minutes here means we miss minutes there. But Sherree was a dream when she was all done up. I remember every dress she ever wore. That night it was a sky blue short and stretchy affair with a sequin border around the sleeves and hemline teamed with my favourite shoes; they were red and spangly and clicked when she walked.

When Marc from Glamour Puss walked onstage that night, it was like God had just appeared on Earth. He was gold lamèd up to the neck and bathed in a pool of light so intense we had to blink to see him, and he was singing about the brotherhood of friendship and funk freedom and no more war and by the end no one, not even the bar staff, said a word.

We danced afterwards, Sherree and me. When she gets going she can't stop. "That's what my customers sometimes say," she always said. "Snip snip here, snip snip there. I never know when to stop. A man comes in for a trim and he gets a crew cut. I never know when to stop and it's going to get me in big trouble some day."

Sherree has a natural sense of rhythm. She says she inherited it from her mother, who claims she was Billie Holiday in a former life. When Sherree dances I like to watch her. I love the way she twists her arms and her legs into the most curvaceous of conformations, and the way that even when she shakes her head from side to side, her long, blonde hair flailing all over the place, it still drops down neatly into place before the next song starts. I try to follow her, but it's useless. I don't have the energy, and besides when I dance I just place one foot in front of the other, like a walk that's going nowhere. My arms stay firmly by my sides, cocked at an angle that not does vary with the song. That night I danced for a while and then sloped off to circulate. Half an hour later I was hammered. I'd downed some chasers and Tequila slammers and some rum. I'd been chatting to my old mate Phil for all of two minutes when his attention suddenly wandered from my sparkling conversation. He pointed a finger towards the dancefloor, one that was not cradling a glass. "Look at that," he said, with such enthusiasm that several specks of his saliva landed on my chin.

And by god, I'd never seen anything like it. He was all slicked back supercool hair, in a shirt unbuttoned to reveal a naked chest, teamed with tight lilac bellbottoms, the slinkiest I had ever seen. He was in the centre of the dancefloor, dancing close to Sherree. Phil tapped me on the shoulder and hollered: "He IS the seventies."

STARS IN HER EYES

amy prior

The seventies isn't just about wearing the right clothes, the right make-up, the grooviest accessories. Gold lamé just does not look good on some people. On some people flares just don't hang right. But even if you get the look, you haven't necessarily got the attitude.

The seventies attitude. You've either got it or you haven't. Sherree's got it. Marc from Glamour Puss has got it. And this man, whoever he was, this man in the centre of the dancefloor, dancing with so much cool, this man had so much attitude it radiated from the pores of his skin. The way he smiled, showing the white tips of his front teeth – that was part of it. The way he broke off from dancing, moving slowly and deliberately across the dancefloor to the bar to take a sip from his Bacardi and coke. That was too. And the way, every so often, he clicked his fingers to the beat. He was the real thing alright, and it had nothing to do with the coke.

I took a sip of the vodka Phil had placed in front of me. My stomach was beginning to churn and I realised that I had not eaten since breakfast that morning. By the time I looked up again, seventies man and Sherree had devised a dance routine of their own. Two steps forward, two steps back, with a bit of a hop, skip and jump in between. "He's John fucking Travolta," said Phil, squeezing my shoulder. "He may be fucking John Travolta, but he's dancing with my Sherree," I shouted, but I don't think he heard because his eyes remained fixed on the happy couple.

By the time I decided to confront them on the dancefloor, my stomach felt as if it was about to explode. I imagined that the heat and pressure inside it was so intense that it would ignite the alcoholic cocktail that swam within its walls, making it project out of my mouth all over them. It was not a happy thought.

"What the fuck do you think you're doing here mate?" I said to Travolta. He didn't even notice me, and they carried on with their set routine, which had now incorporated some hip movement. I tapped him on the shoulder. "What the hell are you playing at? This is my girl," I shouted. He turned round, and I realised he was very tall. Well, taller than me. He froze, stared at me with his unblinking blue eyes, but didn't say a thing.

"Jesus, Dave, I'm just having fun," Sherree said, grabbing my arm and leading me away from the dancefloor. "See you around," she shouted to seventies man, waving and smiling in a way I hadn't seen in a while. "How much have you had to drink?" she said to me, frowning. I saw she was developing tiny lines along her forehead. I wondered if he had got close enough to notice that about her.

Sherree got a taxi back and I ended up walking three miles home on my own and woke up on top of my bed the next afternoon wearing only my new white boots, which had somehow become stained chocolate-khaki. Sherree phoned at four. "I'm sorry baby," she said in that sweet voice of hers. I could just imagine her, painted toenails perched up on the kitchen table, perhaps drenching her Rich Tea biscuit in a warm drink until it was soft enough to dissolve in her mouth without her having to bite or chew. "I was just dancing, Dave. You know how I like to dance, don't you?" she said.

But I still couldn't stop thinking about her and him together. In the dimness of my own bedroom, in the half light between work and sleep, I replayed that night again and again in my own head trying to piece together what really happened. How close was he holding her? Close enough, I saw, to touch her hips. And what did this complete stranger say to her that made her laugh in such an animated way? I was so drunk that night, maybe I had missed something more. Maybe they had kissed in a dark corner of the dancefloor. "See you around," I remembered her saying to him. I recalled that very clearly. Did she really plan to see him again, I wondered. When I did ask her about him once, she said nothing for a while and then she just looked at me from under that wispy fringe of hers and said: "Forget it, Dave, forget it," disappearing soon after without a kiss or a promise of when I would see her again.

Something had to change. Maybe, I thought, just maybe if I got more seventies too, then she would have as much fun with me as she did with the stranger. Yeah, I dug the music, but the clothes I wore did not really say seventies big time. So in one week I spent more than fifty pounds in charity shops on wide lapel shirts. I got my hair permed like Marc Bolan. I started to wear a feather boa when we went out. But although I had the right clothes and the grooviest accessories, when it came to attitude I knew the stranger still won hands down.

Staying in simply fuelled my worries. So when I wasn't seeing Sherree, I tried to go out with Gary. Gary was a friend of a flatmate who kept coming round even after his friend had moved out. I think it was a convenient stop between his own house and his dealer's. That's how I got to know him. Nights with Gary were simple, beery affairs in which we talked about nothing much but music.

One night after more than a few jars at the Bull and Gate, we decided to buy some food for the walk home. We had a choice of kebab and pitta or a selection of tuna mix salads at the Doner Delight, but all we really wanted was chips drenched in ketchup. So that's what we told the Greek man and he said: "They'll be a few minutes, is that OK?" and I said: "We're in no hurry mate." The shop was suffused with a white electric glow that made the faces of the drinkers in the queue paler than they already were. It was closing time and place was filling up fast. We squeezed up tight against the counter and tried to look outside the window, but the heat of sweating bodies inside had steamed it up, and there were only drips of condensation to distract us.

"Here's your chips mate." We turned around and I was met by a pair of blue eyes over the counter, a pair of unblinking eyes that sent a pulse of energy through my tired brain. The eyes looked at me for an instant, with a jolt of recognition, and then they focused on Gary.

"Gary. How's it going, mate?" the man said, placing a greasy hand on his shoulder.

"Andrew," Gary said in a surprised tone, "How long's it been? Two years?"

"Is it really that long? What you been up to?" said Andrew.

"I've got a stall at Camden Lock: jewellery, scarves, accessories, that kind of stuff..." said Gary. And they chatted for a while, but not that long because there was quite a queue behind us.

"I think these chips are getting cold," I said to Gary. This seemed to remind him of my presence, and he introduced me to Andrew.

"Yes, we've met before, haven't we?" with a tone in my voice that I fancied was quite dry. His hair was in the same slicked-back style, though perhaps not as bouffant as it had been on the dancefloor, and his lilac bellbottoms were now a green nylon overall.

Andrew was an old friend of Gary's from technical college. They had both studied fashion design, but after the course they lost contact. Gary moved to Ibiza for a while; Andrew stayed in London. When he wasn't at the chip shop, Andrew took dancing lessons from Doris Schwartz, a lady who was reputed to have tutored Hollywood actors on the correct steps.

I learnt all this when we met, at Andrew's suggestion, in a late bar on Highgate Road after he'd finished work. Andrew talked to Gary like they were long lost intimates, and I felt our previous meeting on the dancefloor was best left unmentioned. Besides, my brain was feeling too messed up for confrontation. I couldn't look at him without thinking about Sherree. I looked at his mouth and remembered how she smiled at him. I looked at the way he touched Gary on the shoulder and remembered how I saw him touch Sherree on the hips. I heard him speak and remembered the way she had said so brightly: "See you around." Afterwards we went back to his place.

He lived five minutes from the chip shop in a small one bedroom attic flat in an old Victorian terrace. We sat in his lounge drinking tall glasses of whisky and he talked us through his record collection. I was feeling exhausted, and after a while I was only half listening. It didn't seem to matter much because Gary did most of the talking, and besides, Andrew only needed an occasional nod of the head to reassure him of your interest. I sank down into the orange vinyl sofa

and let my eyes wander around the fabric of the room. On the wall opposite me was a large framed mirror with Travolta superimposed on it, teeth whiter than white. Next to that was a huge chrome-plated drinks cabinet, on which stood a cocktail shaker and a million mixers (all the bottles arranged in neat rows), as well as a variety of glasses: fluted and straight, tumbler and tall. Opposite was a large gold crucifix, perhaps three foot long, encrusted with jewels and a collage of seventies stars (I could see Gary Glitter and Olivia Newton-John).

Then my eyes focused, perhaps for only the second time that evening, directly on Andrew's. He met them and smiled. "Would you like some music?" he asked. I nodded. He ran his fingers through his hair. I wondered if they were still covered in vegetable oil from the chip shop. Maybe that was the secret of his greased-back style?

"Let's hear some Bee Gees," Andrew said.

He crossed the room very slowly over to his tape collection and picked the right one in an instant: "They're alphabetically arranged," he said, by way of explanation. Then, very slowly, very precisely, he lifted the tape out of its box, placed it in his midi system and pressed play. He turned the dimmer switch down to low and walked to the centre of the room. Then I was aware of tiny rectangles of light tracing a circular path around the rug in the centre of the room. "Do you like it?" he said, pointing up at the ceiling. "That's so cool," said Gary, looking at a revolving globe decorated with lots of tiny mirrors. "Where did you buy that?"

And then Andrew began to dance. Slowly at first, but then he loosened up and gave quite a performance. It lasted twenty minutes, maybe more, certainly enough time for him to have freshened up my glass three times. "Come on Dave, come and dance," said Andrew. By this time, Gary was clapping his hands and shuffling his feet from side to side. I was starting to see eight arms and eight legs flailing around the room, so I did not think that joining them was a wise idea.

But Andrew was insistent. "Come on Dave. Come on," he shouted, pulling my arm sharply. I managed to stand up, but had to hold onto the sofa arm to steady myself when I tried to move my right leg back and forth from the knee downwards in time with the beat. After a while, Andrew began to sing into one of the shoes Gary had removed, and he took Gary's arm and they jumped up and down, punching their fists in the air. Then I saw Andrew hold the hem of Gary's T-shirt and slowly begin to roll it up, exposing only his navel at first, but then his stomach, his nipples and the lightest smattering of chest hair. Then he lifted it off completely, gently raising it up his neck and over his head.

I remember thinking that the floor would be a good place to rest for a while, even though at that moment I felt a curious lightness of spirit. I laid out on the rug, my arms spread out wide to steady myself. I closed my eyes, and for a moment I thought I saw Sherree's face. She was looking right at me, from under that wispy fringe of hers, and smiling. When I opened them again, Andrew's face was two inches away from mine. "You are Jesus, David, and I am going to crucify you," he shouted. He grabbed the gold crucifix from the wall and raised it above my head. Then he knocked imaginary nails into the palms of my hands and my ankles. And then he began to sway his hips, clap his hands and move his feet from side to side in between my sprawled-out arms and legs. "Ah, ha, ha, ha staying alive, ah, ha, ha, ha staying alive," he sang again and again, matching Andy Gibb's falsetto tone, and I felt my spirits lift even more as his voice rose up high through the attic window, above the trees and into the sky.

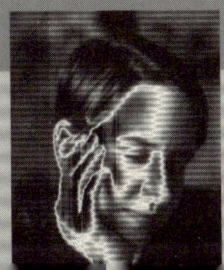

Amy Prior was born in Glasgow, raised in Coventry, schooled in Manchester and now lives in London. She has worked as a frying assistant in a chip shop and as editor of a problems page for a lipsticks and facelifts magazine, among other things.

sugar pool

Phew. Kinda wobbly. It was that floppy, dizzy, dreamy feeling. The debilitating reassurance of coming up on a good pill. I squashed myself onto the edge of a bench at the back of the dancefloor. Now the shoom of the bass and the flashing strobe was partially masked by the happy sweaty mass around me. Alright I said to the boy I'd more or less sat on. He didn't reply, instead he put his hand out tracing the contours of my face. That was kinda cool but it stopped pretty abruptly. Sorry he said, suddenly straightening up, I am sorry, must be a trippy pill. I smiled, looking him straight into his big black eyes. Just coming up myself, what's your name?

Adam.

ad atkins

I'm Jo, are you alright Adam?
Yeah, will you sit with me for a bit while I straighten out.
Sure.
Always happens this.
Me too, I replied.
I've lost me mates.
Yeah, the last I saw of our lot they were in the cloakroom queue. I left my stuff on the coach, hardly worth bringing it in eh?
Where've you come from?
Surrey, not the posh part though.
Oh yeah, I only live down the road, been here before?
Yeah, smart isn't it.

Had some of my best nights ever in this place. Prefer the back room to all that Harage and Gouse.

Yeah me too.

We sat and chatted like you do on the E. His eyes got brighter and bigger, the perspiration on his forehead matted his short dark hair. He looked like a swimmer or a boxer. His mesmerising way of explaining things, all hands, eyes and a huge grin, held me entranced. We got on over and above the normal clubbing niceties. He was really good fun.

Ready for a dance? I asked.

Yeah in a minute, will you come to the food bar with me?

What's all that about then? They don't have a food bar in here do they? You're E'd off your tits and you want to get something to eat! I've heard of disco burgers but this is ridiculous.

No worries, just that I've got to keep an

(77)

eye on the blood sugar and you know, got a bit of a problem with the diabetes, he said in his open, matter of fact manner. It's just one of those things.

    We danced and danced. His happy grin lifted me every time we made eye contact. The music was hard but uplifting. Tonight it sounded clearer and sharper than ever. The room filled with some of the most beautiful sounds that I'd ever heard. We bumped into our mates, dancing together for a while. I ended up losing my girlfriends again when they drifted off into the housey room. We had another one of his E's. I'd never seen one with a horseshoe on the back before but it was really good, got me flying and kept me going for absolutely ages. I lost all track of time. That didn't matter. Things happened even quicker than they usually do when you're on a pill. Tonight more than any other night the lights came up far too early. Adam gave me a really big hug. He said that we'd have to find my mates.

    Try the cloakroom queue eh?

    We did but there wasn't even a queue, certainly no sign of my lot.

    Oh well, I suppose we can wait outside for them, the coach doesn't go until six thirty.

    What! It's gone eight o'clock, this place has got a late licence tonight. Don't worry we'll wait for a bit to see if any of them are still here, I'll help you out with a taxi if the worst comes to the worst.

    We walked to the side of the main doors past the offers of dodgy minicabs and people thrusting club fliers into tired hands.

    Hang on to this a second, he grinned handing me his coat, don't suppose you want anything from the burger van?

Bottle of water if that's alright.

I thought he was winding me up when he asked the man for a doner kebab with lots of strawberry jam. Yuck, absolutely yuck, I teased him.

He handed me my water bottle. I get two of these sometimes but I'm not feeling too bad tonight.

I'm glad to hear it.

We sat on a wall, grateful for the midsummer sun that warmed our damp clothes.

Doesn't look as if they're turning up, do you mind if I come back to yours for a bit?

Are you sure? he asked with the first hint of reticence that I'd detected all night.

Yeah, I'm still buzzing and it doesn't really feel like the night's over yet. I certainly don't feel like spending the next hour or so in one of those decrepit minicabs. You got any decks or anything?

Yeah, I have, as it happens. We'll have to be quiet, though. The neighbours are always complaining about ornaments and things falling off shelves and whatever when I really get it going. 'Bout time I was getting back anyway, I've got to sort out my injections and all that.

Ugh. I don't mean...

Don't worry, it's one of those things. You've just got a healthy distaste for needles and injected drugs. So've I, but I have to rely on them. I'd rather just have a booster like most people but my doctor says my body isn't up to it.

I looked at him and smiled: Looks alright to me.

We bundled ourselves onto a hop on and off bus, jumping off half a mile down the road.

Talk about jealous, my jaw dropped when I saw his flat. I had to put up with my parents so the sight of his living room with masses of vinyl, decks, a couple of synths and things almost took my head off.

I gave him a hug. It lasted forever. I hadn't come back for sex and I'd had the feeling that he wasn't up for it. It wasn't something I was really all that interested in after a night on the E. Nonetheless we stood caressing, taking each other's clothes off before gently falling on a rug in front of his turntables. He jolted uncomfortably when I stroked his limp dick.

Undeterred I moved my hand back. Don't worry, I've heard it's hard to get it up when your E'd up or speeding.

He smiled uncomfortably so I concentrated on kissing him.

Are you sure you're ready for this? he asked me after what seemed like an age.

Yeah.

I'll just go and get a thingy then.

Cute, I thought as I watched his sporty arse disappear out of the door. I went to take a drink from my water bottle. Empty. So I went out the door to find the kitchen or bathroom assuming that he'd gone into the bedroom. I ended up in a bedroom so I walked back to where he'd gone.

I retched when I saw what he was doing. I'd never seen anything like it. He had his dick in one hand, pulling it down. The other hand held a big syringe which he seemed to be discharging into a faint blue vein. Shocked at being disturbed he tried to hide what he was doing.
I staggered back into the living room and started screaming. I tried to put my clothes on. He ran after me trying to hold me but I wasn't having any of it. It's alright, he said trying to hold me.

Just fucking get off me! It's disgusting. If you think that I am going to sleep with a fucking smackhead then you can fuck yourself, you fucking weirdo!

He stood there, limply crying before slumping into a chair.

I mean to say, what type of addict injects himself in the dick! Got no other veins left eh, junkie? All this shit about blood sugar, think I'm fucking stupid or something?

It's not like that, he sniffed.

Yeah. Course it isn't. I've heard junkies are the best liars in the world and I am not hanging around to hear any more tall tales.

Really, I'm not lying to you. Look at the label.

I wasn't interested as he tried to show me a couple of ampoules.

It's the diabetes. Doesn't happen to everyone. I was alright until about a year ago but now I've got to inject this to get it up. Seriously.

It was the sad twinkle in his eye. I could see that he was telling the truth.

Why didn't you say then? You're supposed to be open and frank on E, tell people what you really feel, be honest and tell the fucking truth.

I've tried that before but no one wants to stay around to find out. Trouble is that I really like you and I just didn't think any of this was going to happen tonight. It's all come on a bit quick.

There were still tears in my eyes but I could feel a smile breaking out. So you do what then? I asked, taking the syringe from his hand. You shoot this up and then it's ready for action?

Yeah, look I'll show you if you're interested, he said, regaining his composure.

I was interested. Fascinated, as it happened, but that could wait. I put my arms round him. I'll do that for you in a couple of minutes. Just let me make up for flying off the handle. We cuddled and stroked each other and fell back onto the rug in front of his turntables. I looked into the same big black happy eyes that had mesmerised me all night. I was glad that I hadn't gone home. I felt kinda wobbly. Phew. It was that floppy. It was that, dizzy, dreamy feeling. This time it wasn't the pills loving me up.

AD Atkins's first novel, *Ecstasy, sorted and on one*, was published in 1996. He is currently working on a sequel.

I was on the ground.
And then I was in the air.
And now I am under the water.

night swimming

1

Everybody knows that water is blue, but then this isn't real water, I guess. Night water. What gets left in a pool when you drain the daylight away. Between dawn and dusk, I have watched the sun polish this piece of water: laminations of swiftsilver at noon, smarting like brass in the evening. The moon floating in it, a pickled egg in a pint of stout.

    We dropped out pre-club and came instead to where the dark stuff creeps its way right up into the centre of it all. Jamie's here, crouched on the edge with his knackered old 80s boom box whacked up full, head dipping in time to the deep dum-dum beats. A waxing moon, the warehouses' high

jonathan gibbs

wattage security spots—it's a class venue. The towpath running along one bank is a public right of way, but god knows no one comes here after dark, except the odd weirdo out walking their dog. The acoustics are great: you get a double, triple echo off of the blank flats of the warehouse walls facing off across the thin trench of water, giving the slack, looping bass a wicked touch of reverb.

We're here to play the torch game. The torch is on the ground by Jamie's feet. A big, battery-sucking daddy with a carrying handle, powerful enough to pick off passing planes, just about.

And waterproof, of course. I stretch off my shirt and step out of my pumps, treading down the heels. Stand there a moment, curling my toes on the ledge and swinging my arms down at my sides. Listening, and trying to forget to listen. I slide off my shorts and then I'm gone.

I aimed for the moon, but could not tell if I hit it— I always close my eyes when I dive. I hit water, rolled and kicked and let my body subside; past the first punch of sensation, when it's neither hot nor cold, just extreme. Move internally only, and to the given rhythm, felt from a distance. You enter into it easily, and stay there; it's like watching the regular rise and fall of telephone wires out the window of a speeding car. My mouth chock full of greasy upside air; I seep it out globule by globule. It stretches, balloons and slips

away sideways from my lips.
    Then the surface imploded and the torch came spinning and dropping by me like a shot-down spaceship. I burrowed downwards, frogkicking and groping with my arms, heaving silted liquid out the way, straining my fingers after the rotating shaft of dimming bright; to touch the dark bulk I knew was there behind the beam, but couldn't see. I punished the water before me with aching and flailing arms. The torch hit bottom and the beam stopknocked and pointed back at me; but my breath was gone and my lungs ready to give out. I curled and tucked and pushed back for the surface like a swimmer doubling back at the end of the pool. Tuck and turn.

And then I was under the water. And now I am in the water. But the water is upside-down or sideways, up is not where I left it, and either the seal was fucked or something, but the torch is all of a sudden gone. No lights, no signposts. I fancy I can still make out the submarine dub modulations of the bass way down here, but it's not coming from any one direction.

    This is where I get a rush—thrash—dance like a got fish. I gulp in fright and take water into my mouth. A connection made and immediately broken. Tracing a possible intimacy. I had opened, and then sealed over. This confiscated, annexed area of water in my mouth... blueprint of a kiss.

And Jamie squatted still but for the slow rhythmic roll of his haunches. Watching, listening, mouth hanging slightly open. Nostrils flaring in time. Nodding, as if to say: Yeah, okay, sure—this is cool. There's nothing to be worrying about here,

And so now, and now, and now I was inside the water. There had been a folded opening, a fault in the continuum, and I had glided in and been ingested. Everything just gone. Skipped. Water unbound by air or earth or walls. I choked and swallowed and gagged on the water. It was heavy like a quilt. Tight like blankets. Cool like sheets.

   Now, of course, I understand. I've seen it, and I know. All canals, rivers and streams, lakes and lochs, pools and ponds and puddles: they all come together underground. The expanse of surface water is but a fraction. They link arms and digits, fingers slit into finger hinges, searching out like negative roots the shared parentage of limestone caverns, underground river systems, networks of sewage channels built by the Romans, by the Picts, by earthworms. Subterranean aqueducts. Horizontal waterfalls. One day the era of erosion will be complete, and Britain will be a floating island, poised on a tidal lake of all waters.

And so I was in the water. And then I was beyond the water.

Someone hugged me. There was a crush of arms about my head and chest and the warmth and force of a human body against mine and it felt good. I grinned and tried to hug back; the next thing I knew someone was kissing me, and I was dying, backwards.

   My body shook and a face appeared. God's face swam above me. God with a greying black bob and wide eyes in a face that took in the whole horizon. When she pounded my shaking chest and blew new life into the cave of my ribs, salt tears crashed down on my eyeballs, wetter than the stuff on me and in me. Next, the familiar sound of an ambulance—the most comforting sound in the world, I've always thought, when you grow up in a city. The homely blue strobe. Jamie's hand tugging at my elbow. Telling me I'm gonna

85

be all right, or it's gonna be all right. I shivered in my skin. At night, the water is warmer than the air outside it. Anyway.

Somewhere along the line, the torch beam had melted into a strip, a long tooth of light, hungbar above me, below me. I orbited it and was still. It came and went, curdled purple and green anemones and galactic swirls on the inside of my eyelids, even at darktime. For yes, there was dark. And light. Like a clown who swipes a smile from his face with the flat of his hand, and restores it as it rises. And dark again. And light.

So now I know.

The human body floats or sinks. Depending on where it is. Where it's in or on. It will not roll out of a canal. It will not float calmly up from the depths of a bed. There it can sink and sink and never come to rest. This I know, then: what I have learned. That drowned bodies are happier than buried ones. Their fluids and liquids (sixty-six per cent) sigh as they slip back into the embrace of the water, rather than be sucked at by the thirsty roots of trees.

This I have seen: a celebration of water. Stalactites in cavernous limestone cathedrals drip in an ongoing devotional, clustered in groups of varying lengths and slendernesses. And stalagmites, intercessionary candles that grow, as they burn. Not extinguish into a mean puddle of wax. The sound of water falling is the sound of prayer, of patience, and of faith. Echoed into the farthest corners of the darkness, illuminating and delineating the space. The echo of each drop measures the extent, the shape of the silence that it breaks.

And so now I was beyond the water. The water was behind me.

Although I sometimes dreamed that the white bed I slept on was a raft, precisely balanced on the surface of an ocean that dropped away far below me in a sickening, terrifyingly two-

dimensional verticality.
I would wait for the leak that would eventually come, seeping warm, Caribbean water into the sheets and spreading fingers out under my sleeping body. The bed would become heavy, heave and give, start to dip.

Other times the raft held and I washed up awake dry.

Other times. Elsewheres. Water under ground.

I woke with a start and found a spray of flowers leaping at me, all leaning in a frozen motion of curve. The stems like speed marks, the residual images carved on my retinas. The flowers were very bright. They sat in a clear cut-glass vase, and I watched the slanted cut stems suckle and slurp. I watched the bubbles cling to onto the inside of the glass. I thought about myself, drowning, in the canal. I wondered if they liked being bubbles, or if they felt trapped, wanted to become air again. They must like it, I decide, because sometimes they stay down there for ages. Some of them. How long can a bubble hold its breath?

I woke and watched the strip light, closed my eyes and still felt its presence. Felt the refracted heat off the white walls. Pushed back the blanket and dipped my toe gingerly onto the floor, testing its warmth. Testing whether it would take my weight.

Then a woman was there, I could sense her fidgeting beside the bed as I eddied onto the shore of waking, undecided like a snatch of driftwood, bobbing in and out. I rolled over and worked the muscles in my back, and felt a body leap to attention, hands on handbag clasp on knees, leaning forward. I slitted my eyes and watched the dark and yellow form itself into the sitting figure of my mother. Leaning in along with the flowers.

Darling, oh thank God. Harry, he's awake, come

quick. Darling, how do you feel? She withdrew a hankie from her sleeve and attempted to force it back in through the corner of her eye.

And Dad was next to her, in that strange pose from old black and white photographs. Stood behind and to one side of her, hand placed on her shoulder. It pressed and squeezed, four flat fingers. My vision started to give at the edges, whiten. Just like in old photos. Her hand reached up unseeing and rested on his, resting on her. That was a nice touch, I thought.

You're lucky to be alive, my boy, he said, and she nodded.

As if I owed it to them personally.

Next time I woke, they were resolved unto a nurse and it was sheet changing. I sat in a new bathrobe in a chair and pigeoned my feet and watched him from behind my eyelashes. Wished I had a pair of dark glasses. Or some magazines or anything. He wrinkled his nose and I looked at my toes. I was really hungry and said so, so they brought me a cup of tea and a currant bun.

I looked for a clock on the walls, but there wasn't one. My digital watch was on my little bedside cabinet, but it wasn't water resistant—its LCD all silted up, layers of sludge under glass like a souvenir.

Mum and Dad came back with more flowers—the other ones had lost their impetus, started to decelerate and fade. They brought grapes and oranges and a nurse produced a bowl and they put them in it on the bedside cabinet, which was cool, because at home we only had tinned fruit ever.

When Dad went out for a fag, Mum sat on the edge of the bed and smoothed the blanket like she used to do when we were both younger, patted my hand and said how scared they'd all been and concerned and then she paused and patted and examined the liver spots on the back of her hand and then she asked what I had been doing.

I said that I had taken drugs and gone swimming naked at night in the canal, and I'd been with Jamie only Jamie can't swim, can he, and this woman was out walking her dog... but by then she'd slipped from the bed like it was high up, and had walked fast out of the ward, looking like she was going to be sick, only she was holding her hand over her forehead, not her mouth.

I wasn't worried, because I knew everything would end up all right and she would come back in soon, with or without Dad, and she would tell me she forgives me and she'd cry and hold my hand and hug me and avoid my eye and then they'd drive home and watch Casualty, probably.

I threw back the covers and shivering scooted out for a slash, feet cold on the floor, cold. I pissed, shook, and then, thinking guilty thoughts about Mum, and about how they're your parents and you should be thankful for them, really, ran a basin of hot, to wash my hands.

I'm there now.

Standing here, in the toilet in a hospital that suddenly I realise I can't situate, geographically. That I've been in for I don't know how many days, hours. Hands held on the rim of the porcelain or whatever, looking down at me looking up. I have been my reflection, I am thinking. I look at my reflection. It looks scared. It's okay, I tell it, without speaking, I know. I've been there. I know.

Jonathan Gibbs was born in 1972. He is a sometime *Scotsman* critic and junk mail stooge. Lives in Balham, does all the usual stuff. No previous offences.

Andi was a good record producer, a producer of rock'n'roll records, a tall German with long black hair which hung down between his broad shoulder-blades.

Most of the time he wore black leather trousers and the t-shirts you'd expect a Ramones fan to wear. Leather trousers don't suit most men, but Andi was thin enough to carry it off.

judgment night

Joe Ambrose

Andi heard the *Judgment Night* soundtrack when he briefly moved back to Berlin in 1993. The fusion of rock and rap, his two favourite musics right then, wrapped him up in the CD. The pirate radio station in Berlin played it all the time through that bleak winter.

Andi had grown bored of the music he'd been doing in London through the late 80s, doomed projects conceived vampirically between Tottenham Court Road and Old Compton Street. *Judgment Night* filled him with shiny modern, untried, ideas. The grunge of Biohazard plastered onto the rap of Onyx. Phallic Helmet and indigenous Slayer versus geek Sonic Youth and venal Mudhoney.

Andi had quit Berlin in '86 for a slick London rock life which opened up to him when he did a first album for Subliminal Kids, a German punk band who eventually got an American record deal which led to an album produced by a guy who used to work with Alice Cooper. Andi helped make lots of good music in London at first, polishing up the songs of young boys who wanted to be stars. But his own star faded and in '88 and '89 he was back working with garage bands and degenerate line-ups of dinosaur onetime-superstar acts. That was how he met his guitar boy—in a Brixton garage band.

He returned to Berlin with this 17 year old American guitarist he'd gotten to know in a Brixton squat. They had an intense and cold relationship based around oral sex; Andi relaxing, the boy working. Andi was a nice fellow, but not all that nice.

He used to say: "Being nice is not very important anymore. Everybody is nice." Like most people with music business status, he did sex with men and women.

He got a winter of Berlin blowjobs out of his American friend, he took a lot of new drugs at free parties, he got to talk in German again, and his ears checked out the new Berlin music made by the children of Kraftwerk and Can.

BERLIN

He liked his American guitar star, a college educated kid who used words Andi had to look up in dictionaries. They never got to see the *Judgment Night* movie but the CD soundtrack—which the whole world heard that year—was the intimate personal soundtrack to their Berlin sojourn.

It didn't last forever but it was good while it did last. The kid proved himself to be a man and an American, with all the brutality that those qualities implied. Andi, for once, had bitten off more than he could chew. He got pissed off with Berlin anew when the sex caught a plane back to New York. He missed all his stuff (his music, his clothes, his books), which he'd put in a storage unit near Heathrow Airport before abandoning London. So, after 9 months in Berlin, he went back to England.

LONDON

April of '97 Andi was living alone in a large warehouse space on a deserted backstreet near Mount Pleasant Post Office; the lonely commercial zone. He had all his possessions in order around him, milestones or tombstones of achieved or thwarted ambition. On his 34th birthday he went to somebody else's party in Soho. He was heading home at 5 in the morning, buzzing with cocaine, when he saw a Biohazard poster freshly pasted onto a wall. The wallpaper paste looked and smelled like sperm. The group were playing in London in 3 weeks time. His mind flashed back to Berlin, he was briefly emotional, and his befuddled brain recalled Biohazard breaking on through to the other side while a musician sucked his cock on wet afternoons.

Andi went to the ticket bureau the following morning and picked up a ticket. The woman in the ticket booth told him it was selling out fast.

The day of the gig he got up in the very late afternoon. After showering he listened to the messages on his answering machine. A French girl—Lulu—he'd met at a party wanted some advice on record producers. His mother hoped he was keeping well and when was he going to appear in Berlin again? A guitarist from a band wanted him to work on some demos with them.

First he called his mother and talked with her for

20 minutes. She talked to him about her money problems and about how she was bored. He returned Lulu's call and she was pleased to hear from him. They arranged to meet for a drink in the 2 Floors bar in Soho at 8 that evening. He'd go straight to the Biohazard gig from there. He didn't return the call about the demos; he didn't want to do demos anymore.

Before catching a bus into town he smoked 4 pure grass joints and dropped a tab of acid. By the time he got to 2 Floors he was mellow and calm. The bar was semi-busy. 4 younger businessmen in expensive fashionable suits with uniformly cropped hair occupied the big leather couch right inside the front door. At other tables men and women from radio stations and advertising agencies mingled, looking self-important and decisive. The men were macho, the ladies feminine. A tall woman in a black suit talked on her mobile phone while inspecting the free postcard stand. Andi strolled through the bar, bland drum'n'bass filling the air, until he saw Lulu sitting in an armchair positioned up against the back wall. Lulu was short with mousy blonde hair cut tomboy style. She looked a little like Hilary Clinton, just a lot younger. Andi and Lulu talked for an hour solid. She wanted to work on some new electronic music ideas she had. She said she'd done that kind of thing in Paris and San Francisco in her previous incarnations.

Lulu was new to town, she knew about 3 other people besides Andi, he seemed to know the ropes, people said some of the records he did sold real well. He drank Diet Coke and she drank spring water; they were adults who had seen wilder days, and Andi didn't like to mix drugs with drink. They talked about groups they both liked and ridiculous situations they'd gotten into in the music business. He suggested some indie record labels, some people, DJs, other players. If she rang him in the morning he'd have some numbers she could call about cheap studios and duplicating services.

At 9.35 Lulu was heading towards Oxford Circus Tube Station. Andi was walking up the steps leading into the Astoria where Biohazard were about to walk onstage. Inside the venue youth mayhem was breaking loose. Lights were pumping the senses and guitars were manipulating the brains. It took Andi about 3 minutes to walk through the crowd and reach the mosh pit right in front of the stage. Up there the kids were packed in tight on top of one another. By the time the band did *Judgment Night*, about 5 songs into their set, Andi was vaguely recalling Berlin, becoming a part of the human fellowship.

Police were called by the bouncers who'd hauled Andi out of the mosh pit. 7 black bouncers surrounded him and pushed him into the backstage area. All 7 were psycho and twitchy from cocaine and crack. The worst of them, a dreadlocked 7 foot Yardie, kept taking off his sunglasses to rub cocaine-induced tears from his red eyes.

"You bludklat bastard. You do a filthy thing like that! They should kill you, motherfucker! You worse than a killer!" he screamed.

A boy, accompanied by a man in a long expensive overcoat, was brought in front of Andi.

"Is this the man who assaulted you?" the man in the overcoat asked the boy.

"Yes," said the boy.

Andi couldn't see his accuser's face clearly. The light was shining in his eyes.

"Do you want to press charges?"

"Yes."

The boy withdrew. 10 minutes later the cops arrived and took Andi, handcuffed, away from the gig. To the best of his knowledge, Andi had never seen this boy before.

Andi stared out the car window at the people passing by, celebrating a rainy Friday night in the narrow Covent Garden backstreets. He looked down at his handcuffed hands and over at the young policeman sitting alongside him. The police car came to a halt in front of Bow Street Police Station. A huge electric gate opened up, revealing a big yard illuminated by powerful lamps clamped to the side of the station. The car disappeared inside. He was in captivity. He felt like shit but he was so stoned, so much in shock, that nothing other than his immediate physical surroundings registered. Information was going into his brain like random digital sensation; he knew what was happening but it was like an astral projection experience to him. He felt as if the real Andi was floating, disembodied, over the police car. And the astral Andi was looking on indifferently at what was happening to the handcuffed body in the back seat of the car.

Inside the station they sat him down in front of a reception desk. 2 desk sergeants, 1 a fat bald white guy and the other a 45 year old Asian, sat behind the desk, manning bulky old fashioned computer terminals. The Asian—a tightassed family man with a house out in Zone 6—got to deal with Andi. A young prostitute sat alongside him, occupying the time—and computer—of the other desk sergeant. She was about 16 years old, and she looked sideways at Andi with disbelief or drugged confusion.

"Do you understand why you were brought here?" asked the Asian.

"Yes," said Andi. He found it hard to speak. His throat was dry as the desert.

"You have been arrested for indecently assaulting a boy at the Astoria nightclub."

A young officer emerged from somewhere and leaned over the Sergeant's right shoulder.

"We've just found out that the boy is 14, Sarge," he said in a fake conspiratorial tone. These awful words marched through Andi's head, filling him with unexpected dread and terror. He had moved to a suburb of hell, and he might never escape.

The time of arrest was 10:15. The arresting officer explained that he had gone to the Astoria where he found the accused detained by security staff from the venue. The accused denied the allegation. Did Andi want to see a solicitor at this stage? No. Andi wanted to think about things for himself first. Had he any questions? He just wanted to know how long he'd be there. Because the boy was only 14 and possibly traumatised by the incident, because he might have drink or drugs taken, they couldn't interview the victim until the morning, so they had to advise Andi that he could expect to spend the night there.

95

5 minutes later he was marched to a cell. A young black cop theatrically opened the cell door, ushered him in and, as if they were 2 middle-class chaps comparing notes, commented that it was not exactly salubrious accommodation.

But it was a whole lot better than all those detective novels Andi'd read over the years had lead him to believe. It was clean, it had a toilet, there was no smell, and he was mercifully on his own. A note on the wall said that he could make 1 phonecall, see a lawyer, expect a clean cell on his own unless there were exceptional circumstances, and have clean blankets. 3 meals a day were promised.

He lay down on a rock-hard wooden bed leavened by a thin mattress covered in a sea-blue plastic. Plastic, he thought, because a lot of the guys who ended up there were emitting puke or snot or piss or blood or shit.

For 30 minutes he lay perfectly still, his arms by his side, his eyes closed. The tab of acid was now in full effect, and confusion did battle with common sense. Had he touched a boy? As far as he knew, he could recall every last second of the gig. He'd been watching the band, thinking about the past, caught up in his drugs. People were everywhere and nowhere. The boy was a stranger to him, Andi didn't do things like that. But who knows what happened? When confused, be careful. He'd learned what to do next in crime novels.

He opened his eyes to study the ceiling, looking for hidden surveillance cameras high up. There was nothing visible but he wasn't entirely sure. He worked on the basis that state-of-the-art cameras might well be looking down at him. He got up from his bed, swayed a little, and stumbled towards the toilet. He leaned over the bowl, forced himself to vomit onto his hands, and then spent 5 minutes scrubbing his hands in the toilet's water, flushing and flushing again, looking for the tiniest particles of matter gathered under his fingernails or in between his fingers. He dried his hands on his damp t-shirt and lay down on his bed again.

It was time to speak to a lawyer. Andi didn't have a lawyer or a doctor or an accountant. He lived a low profile life: he didn't pay tax, accept cheques, or sign contracts. He got paid in cash, paid his bills in cash, maintained his home as an autonomous zone. He'd told the desk sergeant he was unemployed, so he knew he'd get free legal aid. He rang his bell, a cop came and asked what he wanted. "Bear with me a while," said the warder indifferently when told that Andi wanted to see a free solicitor.

"Hello," said the duty solicitor down the phone from the comfort of his home as Andi stood uncomfortably in an office, 4 cops staring at him. "I gather that you have been charged with indecent assault. How can I help you?"

"I just want some general advice from you as to where I stand," Andi said feebly, 2 of the cops sniggering at his discomfort and embarrassment.

"It will all be a lot clearer in the morning when the victim has made her statement," said the duty solicitor cheerfully.

"Obviously you don't know a whole lot about the case," said Andi, worried but bemused, "because I'm accused of assaulting a boy, not a girl."

"Yes, well," said the duty solicitor, not missing a beat, "I'm sending a solicitor to speak with you in the morning. Have they taken a statement from you?"

"No."

"Have you taken a drink?"

"You mean of alcohol?"

"Yes."

"No. I don't drink."

"Neither do I. It's supposed to be a blessing but it can be a curse," said the solicitor, conjuring up the unpromising vision of a reformed alcoholic. "It's just that I'd strongly advise you not to be interviewed if you've taken a drink."

"I don't drink," Andi repeated. "Do you think I should have a lawyer present when I'm interviewed?"

"It's your legal entitlement to have a lawyer present when you're questioned."

"I know it's my right," Andi said, alarmed by the merely technical nature of the advice he was getting. "I'm asking you for legal advice. Would you advise me to have a lawyer present when they talk to me?"

"I'd strongly advise you to have a lawyer present."

Time moved very slowly after that. Back in his cell, his mind turned to slightly cracked whimsy. For half an hour he thought about Thin Lizzy, the heavy rock band he'd idolised when he was a kid. He smiled when he recalled a story about his best schoolfriend Jon. When Andi and Jon were 12, they listened to Thin Lizzy all the time. *Live & Dangerous* and *Jailbreak* had been the soundtrack of their childhoods. Then Jon's mother was struck down by a brain haemorrhage. In the midst of her crisis her heart stopped beating for two minutes and, technically, she was dead. When she recovered she told Andi that she had felt herself entering into a long white tunnel, drifting far away from her family and friends, whom she could sense behind her. She was moving forward towards some other place in the distance where there was a bright white light. Out ahead of her, close to the light source, she could hear a sound. The sound of Thin Lizzy guitars! Then her heart started beating again, and she came back to the real world.

The Thin Lizzy story didn't seem all that funny when he took into account the fact that Jon's mother, a kind woman who was very fond of Andi, died of a second brain haemorrhage 3 years after that. Even the singer from Thin Lizzy had died young a long time back in another world. All of his thoughts turned bleak and Andi desperately wanted to call somebody but there was nobody he could make that one personal phonecall to. Should he send for a doctor just to have a conversation with a fellow member of the middle classes? The talk he heard a warder having with a Scottish drunk in the next cell convinced him that it wasn't worth the hassle.

The Scot was obviously lonely too. He was going through the motions of demanding a doctor. The warder wanted a good reason why he should go get this doctor. The drunk said he thought he was going to have a heart attack. But he didn't sound like he meant it, like he was worried about dying, so his request was denied.

Around 5am Andi was just nodding off to sleep when 3 English boys were brought noisily into the cells. He saw nothing but heard everything; their voices told him that they were young prosperous suburban kids, Blur generation boys. They'd been busted for dope possession and neither police nor suspects seemed to be taking it too seriously. "You're not really going to put me in there! I'm totally innocent!" said 1 of the boys. It was a London lark for some out-of-town youths.

They talked to one another for a while, their conversation witty enough and entertaining enough. One of them suggested that at least they should all be locked in the same cell, so they could have a decent conversation. But the noise they made woke up a slow American in for starting a fight in a nightclub. Still drunk he complained for an hour about his arrest. He had done nothing wrong. He had to be at work in the morning. He worked as an electrician on a building site and all work would cease if he wasn't on-site. He would lose his job if he didn't get to work by 7 am. The police were deliberately trying to cost him his job.

The central heating was on full blast and there were no open windows in Andi's cell. He'd read in *Time* magazine that schizophrenics were freaked out by too much heat. He didn't think he was a schizo but he could never sleep in a hot room. He didn't like sharing beds with lovers for the whole night either. When sex was finished he kicked his partner out into the street or headed for home himself. He liked loose-fitting clothes, didn't like wearing jackets, liked walking around, even in the freezing depths of winter, in t-shirts.

He'd lost his chance to sleep, so he lay still, awaiting daybreak. He got up to piss and saw, stuck to the back of his cell door, a promotional sticker for the worst band he'd ever produced. The band eventually sank without a trace—deservedly—and his dawn thoughts concerned 3 terrible weeks he'd spent in the studio with Lords of The Ring, 4 financed cretins in tight jeans.

Food was the final diversion. An officer asked Andi if he wanted breakfast and, when the answer was yes, was he vegetarian? Andi found the political correctness absurd, this concern with the sensitivities of vegetarians. He knew that the night was behind him, that nobody had come into his cell to beat him up, that he would soon enter into either a worse nightmare or instant salvation. In the next few hours he would be released on bail or remanded in custody and sent to Pentonville where his old friend Simon had spent 9 months on remand awaiting trial for armed robbery.

Andi knew that if he went into custody he could be in jail for weeks or months and that he would be treated as a sex criminal—a virtual death sentence. He could be knifed or raped or killed by random accident in Pentonville. Simon didn't say much about it when he got out after doing a year. But within 8 months of his release, Simon killed himself with a deliberate heroin overdose and went to his pathetic South London grave without speaking specifically of what went down, what happened to his mind inside Pentonville.

Breakfast was everything the detective novels said that prison food could be. It came from tins, it was poured onto a paper plate and heated in a microwave. Beans that tasted like yellow pack beans will always taste—watery, but beans. The sausages must have been made from the spinal chords of cows long dead from Mad Cow Disease. The potatoes made the really big impact. Andi reckoned they'd been tinned in time for World War 1. They felt and tasted like rubber, but they smelled like formaldehyde. *Rancid*, he thought, *the greatest rock'n'roll band in the world.*

He wanted to wrap up samples in paper from his pocket so he could show them to his friends later. Then it hit him that he might not be seeing his friends later, there might be no "later" other than a van to Pentonville. Tea was the powdered tea they used to serve on the trains years ago. It was strong and revived him. He was damp from the sweat of the gig, and sweaty from his sleepless night in the hot cell.

His lawyer, Malcolm, showed up an hour after breakfast, a short young Jewish guy in a pinstripe suit. His small brown eyes darted to the right and left, avoiding, at first, direct eye contact. He said he'd had time to look over the boy's statement, handing the 10 page document to Andi.

Malcolm was smart and polite in a middle class way. Andi liked him but didn't know whether to trust him or not. Was he too young? Was he a fag? Was he there merely to pick up an attendance fee? By way of small talk Malcolm explained that he had gone to a lot of rockabilly and rock'n'roll concerts in his student days, when he had had a flat-top. They talked about Jerry Lee Lewis—The Killer—and other notorious characters in the history of popular music.

Malcolm explained what was in the statement—he'd not read it through, they'd be there all day if they read right through it, but he'd scanned it and gotten the gist of it. It said that the boy was 14, that he'd been at the concert with his 2 brothers, 1 of whom was studying medicine in London. The lawyer said that you never knew with these middle class families. Sometimes the parents got all self-righteous and howled for justice. Other times they just wanted to pretend that the whole thing had never happened, and that their boy would be far better off forgetting about it.

"I mean," said Malcolm, "there is nothing very much in this statement. He says you pulled down his fly and gently moved your hand up and down his penis. He doesn't say he tried to stop you. If anybody put their hand down my trousers I'd punch them. He says that it all happened in the mosh pit where everybody ends up touching everybody anyway because it's chaotic and people are packed in like sardines. There are no witnesses other than his brothers who say the kid walked over to them and said somebody had put a hand on his penis. It's your word against his and in England it's not what is true but what is provable that really matters. Somebody was filming the concert so there might be some film but presumably it'll show 300 people jumping up and down together. Then at the end there is all this stuff about how he has never had sex with anybody. That he didn't want this kind of thing to happen to him. That he didn't want to be with a man or a paedophile."

Andi said there was nothing to worry about with the film in any case. All it would show was that he was in the clear. There could be no witnesses of any sort; he'd done nothing. They mulled over every aspect of the situation. The solicitor said that the purpose of the police interview that Andi now had to face was, in theory, to get Andi's side of the story. In fact the police would try to get him to confess. It was unlikely they would get overbearing in any way and, in any case, Andi should not under any circumstances react to provocative statements that they might make. They might say Andi disgusted them or that if they had their way they'd lock him up and throw away the key.

Most likely, the matter would eventually be dropped: "14 year old boys make notoriously bad witnesses. Like, what was he doing there in the first place? Why didn't he protest when he felt the hand on his fly? With all these people touching each other everywhere, with the chaos and everyone packed in like sardines, how could he possibly tell who was touching him? If anybody was touching him. You don't have a record of any kind so it's your word against his."

Malcolm told him that the interview with the CID would probably last 20 minutes, that he'd then be released on police bail. This was the big news Andi wanted to hear. Everything else glided by him in a haze. He was older than when he'd been in trouble with police before. The dark looming tunnel of possible incarceration was just another such tunnel, equal to, but no worse than, loneliness or aging, nothing compared with death or illness. He knew life was bad in any case, that music and the drugs that went with his lifestyle were bright sunny days on an otherwise bleak landscape.

The interview was conducted by two cops, one senior and judgmental, one young and unpleasant. Andi denied everything, he didn't speculate on why the boy had picked him out from all the men at the concert to blame for the incident. He had never had a sexual experience with another man. He sometimes went to concerts on his own, sometimes he went with others. It was all some big misunderstanding.

As Malcolm had predicted, the interview lasted 20 minutes. It never got out of hand. The police didn't get ratty or aggressive. Their attitude to Andi seemed to be that he had done it, but that they'd never be able to prove it. They were just going through the motions. They'd kept him in the cells overnight to give him enough of it. He had been punished.

"Would you like to go have a coffee?" Malcolm asked, when they finally got out onto the street.

"Thanks." Andi smiled gratefully. It was nice that his lawyer was happy to break bread with him. "But I just want to get into a fucking taxi, go home, have a shower, and go to bed."

They parted—their secret opinions of one another intact—into the fresh Covent Garden morning. Andi looked around for a taxi but all he saw, in his personal confusion, were coffee shops that wouldn't be opening on Saturday, and newsagents who hadn't opened just yet. His sense of direction was all shot out so he walked aimlessly into a misty rain. He'd walked about 200 yards when he was overcome with the most sublime elation. He was out of captivity, he was walking lightly on the street, breathing in the cold fresh morning air.

A taxi came slowly around the corner, emerging from a back alley. Andi hailed it, a sober morning citizen going about his city centre business. The fat old Jewish driver pulled over onto the footpath and took him off the street. He drove in the direction of Andi's apartment, complaining about how bad business was for that time of year. 5 minutes later the taxi came to a halt again, right in front of Andi's block.

The first thing he did when he got into his sitting room was press the PLAY button on his CD player. Music from a long time ago blared out of the speakers. The madness of the day replaced the madness of the night.

Joe Ambrose is a member of rai-hop terrorists Islamic Diggers who've collaborated with John Cale, Bill Laswell, Anita Pallenberg, and Marianne Faithfull. He organises clubs including *1001 Nights* and *DREAMACHINES*.

The liver should pour out two pints of liquid bile into your bowels daily. If this bile is not flowing freely, your food doesn't digest. Your whole system is poisoned and you feel sour, sunk, and the whole world looks punk.

Adam j Maynard

YUNG

As we ride on the backs of giant flying turtles through the beautiful sparkling night, Casper turns to me. We've both had maybe a few too many drinks and are feeling a little bleary eyed; but the cold, fresh air continues to invigorate as we fly over the glittering streets of Tinseltown. I haven't felt like this for years. This is like feeling young again. Cheerful. The giant wings of the turtles flap away, almost silently. A warm glow rushes through me. I dribble on my patterned shirt. Never mind, it doesn't matter.

My body is knackered by last night's alcohol session. I've been shaking really badly. My fingers won't stay still. I feel nervous, paranoid even. Give me trees. I need greenery! The lines of

LIVER

whizz I did are making me feel jittery. I can't face outside at the moment. I hope nobody comes 'round. I can't speak to anyone right now. My body is pickled, Kraukus gherkins. "Mr Gherkin, how can I help?" My lungs are a refinery. People have been stubbing fags out on them all night. My throat has been slit on the inside with a scalpel. I hate this fucking place. I really do. Swiss mountains on a postcard. That's where I want to be.

Toy, plant, record, salt, high-heeled shoe. I turn on the television. 'The picture wireless' my divinity teacher used to call it. What a wanker, eh! It's the usual mind numbing turd on the box, but I opt to watch it anyway. What else is there to do in this state? Later on I manage to discover an old Peter Cushing thing, and I sit and watch it. Glowing suits, miniature talking robotic dolls, young schizophrenic women, absurd haircuts, crazy music. The main character gets knocked off. It ends. I make coffee. Shallow breathing, thick head. The toy on my mantelpiece winks at me: I'm not kidding!

                              Freaky, man.

After hours.

A sensation overtakes you.

In one of those rare moments of instinct brought on by silent streets and the tingling of aircooled sweat as it blisters on your forehead, released from the tyranny of electric blue PVC and mother of pearl snakeskin, dehydration takes hold and ironwool-tongued you dive for the nearest cafe.

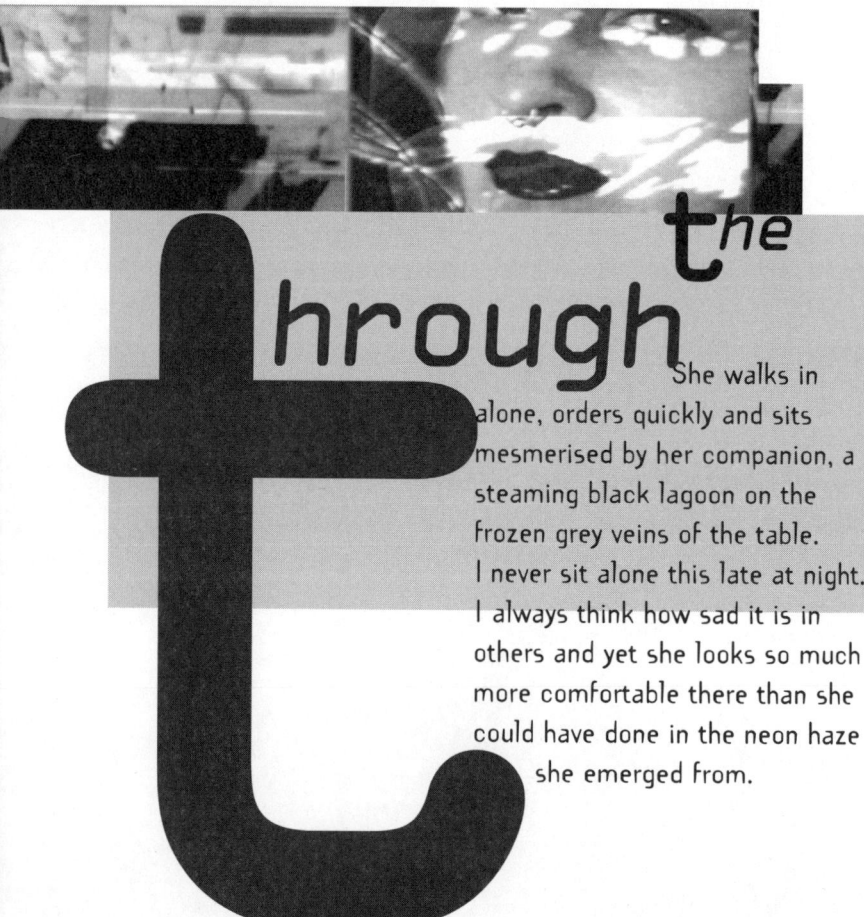

through the

She walks in alone, orders quickly and sits mesmerised by her companion, a steaming black lagoon on the frozen grey veins of the table. I never sit alone this late at night. I always think how sad it is in others and yet she looks so much more comfortable there than she could have done in the neon haze she emerged from.

looking glass

elinor hodgson

Through the tropical tendrils of the token plant and the silhouette of the Eiffel Tower of pepper pots, a red carnation, a black suit, dark hair, a rough complexion. Al Pacino sits opposite her in perfect symmetry. He's been there longer, his cup is empty, its froth sculpted to the rim. She looks up. He hasn't noticed her. She arranges herself, glancing through the shady mirror into the other half of the restaurant and at the weeping mascara in the corner of her right eye. She takes her 60p classic from her mini rucksack and tries to look sophisticated, academic, intriguing. Young studious girl seeks handsome, Italianate, older man, richer, self-contained, enigmatic.

She immerses herself in her book and waits. He is intrigued. He watches as her face relaxes into the print, no longer conscious of his presence as it was before. He walks past her. She looks up. Is he going? No, he walks back to his table and speaks to a waitress who hurries to the bar. He's asked her to get a drink for the girl opposite him. She waits.

No, he hasn't.

She looks away. He's not going to leave without acknowledging her. She rummages in her rucksack and grimaces as she finds what she is looking for, a biro, of unknown colour, the top lost after first removal, the plastic plug at the end chewed over a blank computer screen. She picks the grit from behind her nails, the chocolate crumbs, and whatever else has collected in the depths of her bag, and starts to write inside the cover of her classic, to write about the situation she is in at the moment, perhaps to hand to him when he leaves, or before. She looks up. Level with her fractured red biro, she sees the glint of gold. Maybe he knows she is writing to him and he is writing to her. Maybe he thinks she is writing to a lover and is trying to tempt her away. Perhaps he does not think of her at all.

She's been leaning her head on her elbow, but her arm is shaking too much now. She looks down at her shirt, moulded to her by the evening, except where it gapes where her buttonhole has stretched and the button strayed. She rearranges herself and looks up at him again. Denim clad figures cut the the meniscus of their world, but only momentarily. The lights have gone up a bit, the music changed tempo. People populate the surrounding tables, moving furniture to accommodate sprawling leather and American Tan limbs. The staff sweep past on the aisles. Voices high pitched on second wind dissect the night—yet they are alone together, writing, closeted in a perfect chamber of terracotta tiles.

It's getting lighter outside too. The street lights are starting to look redundant. She packs up to go, catches his eye and pauses. Now is his chance. Is he writing to her? Is he not hurrying now? Does he hear the echo of his childhood nightmare—"Your time is up. Finish the sentence that you are writing and put down your pens"? As she shuffles her belongings together and puts them in her little rucksack he changes position in he seat. Is he rising?

No.

A waitress comes to give her the bill and stands over her as she fumbles with her purse. When her card returns glinting, icy under the spotlight she labours over the signature, trying to make it legible enough to be read if he should happen to ask her name, not that she is in the phone book. She puts a handful of change onto the silver dish and then, as she stands, struggles to pick out the insulting coppers which cling to the smooth brightness. She tucks the chair under the table, smiles with lowered eyes and walks out of the restaurant without looking back.

I put down my pen for a moment and stare at the empty table, as one of the girls adds Sarah's receipt to the pile by my hand.

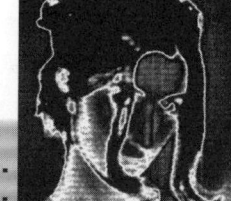

Elinor Hodgson was born in 1973. This is her first published work.

Lisa falls face down on the tarmac again.

There is blood on her nice clothes and her nice face and her average shoes. Jamie is dragging Ed by the wrists from the flaming wreck of Lisa's car. There's not much left of his face. Lisa takes one tiny look at it and she's screaming again.

LISA DRIVES HOME

Alistair Gentry

The night begins in a dark place which has opted out of the clock that the rest of the world operates on. The ceiling is so low that you can reach up with your arms and drag your fingers gently through the sweat that has condensed there.

If nondescript is a description, then that's what the building is. Two delicately-boned girls who look like they're barely old enough to leave school kiss each other gently on the lips. Delirious bodies and flickering lights, endless beat and sternum vibration. After getting groped by security and being given the green light, Jamie looks for Ed and Kerry and as if responding to a dog whistle there they are, answering his unheard call and emerging from the seething overstimulated rabble to shout into his face things that he still doesn't understand even after they've been repeated three, four, five times.

Lisa appears in a cloud of Light smoke, looking delightfully sluttish, her intriguing overbite sidelit to perfection by the bar to her left. Tonight she is unpredictable, verging on hostile, and pisses Jamie off in a number of non-specific ways. Ed disappears for a while and then returns holding his forehead and saying he's just been punched in the face by someone on E, and he doesn't really get over the shock all night. On the wall, blurry slides flash things like HOMO, WHORE, GO-GO, CUNT, DEALER, QUEEN, FUCK and although it is probably not what they are for, these words describe the patrons very well.

They are swallowed and laid claim to by the crowd, absorbed like little white pills, and they don't have to be independent any more. They are looking at each other, feeling the heat and the concourse of people. The sensations of surface and edge. Running eager innocent hands over fabric and feeling exquisitely the difference when they encounter flesh, soft and pliable or stiff and rigid.

A pack of the worst-looking drag queens any of them has seen in living memory arrive. As the queens sashay straight across the dancefloor, their x-large tits bob alarmingly; like pairs of fighting kittens are trapped in their short little tight spangly dresses. It is at this point that Jamie, Lisa, Ed and Kerry leave, emerging into the street and staggering from the silence after hours of intense unrelenting sensation.

—Why why why? Lisa is hysterical and Jamie feels compelled to slap her. He does it so hard that she falls over and lands on her backside, sits down abruptly on the kerb, stunned. Jamie puts his hands up on either side of his head. He is thin and needs a shave. He's got a TV tan, sallow and set off by horn rims. He rarely sees the light of day except when it's coming or going. Takes Ed's hand in his. Listens to the wrong side of Ed's chest but it doesn't matter because the heart is silent and still now anyway, then puts his hand over Ed's mouth to see if he is breathing and he's not. The air is thick with burning petrol. Above the smear of orange light the sky is empty and blueblack except for a thin column of rising smoke.

Lisa lights a cigarette on autopilot and momentarily, irrationally, thinks of lighting it from the burning car like she does from the gas rings at home, then she remembers how she always catches a few stray strands of hair in front of her face alight and the vile smell of singed hair, the only thing worse is the smell of burning meat and she absolutely does not want to think about that.

Jamie kneels and starts to thump Ed hard on the chest with childlike fists. Memories of first aid lessons of a decade ago, cursory and little attended to in the first place, buzz now half remembered in his brain.

——Breathe!

Jamie kneels beside the body and Lisa just stares with smeary panda pisshole eyes and smokes. He suddenly, furiously, aims his fists at Ed's chest again.

——Breathe!
(THUMP)

Lisa croaks something which she herself can't understand because her vocal chords have been shocked into disobedience and they make the words come out wrong.

——Breathe!
(THUMP)
——Breathe!
(THUMP)
——Breathe!
(THUMP)

——You bastard.

Lisa staggers over to stand behind Jamie. She informs him that in her opinion Ed is probably dead, and if he wasn't before he certainly is now.

Jamie's blows are drained of all energy but they continue for a while regardless until both hands eventually succumb to inertia and lie still on Ed's chest. Lisa smokes her cigarette down to the filter and starts another. Jamie kicks Ed's body hard and it makes a hollow meaty sound. He slaps the cigarette, which Lisa has just lit, out of her mouth. It's something about the way she stands there with her coat falling halfway down her shoulder that moves him to do it, and the momentary stinging of the palm of his hand, the slight give of her cheek, somehow makes him feel better. She crawls along the ground after the cigarette, grovels by the side of the empty black road after her grip on sanity.

111

She feels completely alone, completely alone, completely alone, her face two feet from the road, laying on her side. One hand holds the cigarette which she has recovered, the other hugging her thin self tightly. She wants to build a box around herself. There's just that one word—why?—hovering before her, branded into her retinas like a glimpse of the sun. There is warm liquid blood in her eyes. Supermodels smoke Marlboro Lights. She read that in a magazine once. So does she.

Jamie puts his jacket over Ed's face. He is not sure why, but he thinks that it is the done thing and anyway who wants to look at an object like that laying in the road? In his other hand he holds a large soft drink container. He mindlessly sucks insipid, flat Fanta through the straw as he stares for a long time at his friend's legs and spastic grasping nothing hands protruding out from under the coat. It isn't real. He just keeps waiting for the drama to end, for the commercials to begin. Ed who told him that if he was a girl he'd go out with him, definitely. Ed who was cheeky and just went up and said hi and started being very familiar with the girls who'd had something to drink or put on their tongues. Ed who had a stunted sense of personal space and a CD player but only five CDs. Now there's nothing in that silent little grey kingdom of meat.

This is not exactly what he wanted from his Saturday night. He really did not need Lisa to crash the car. He didn't say, Lisa it's Saturday night so let's get shitfaced on brands of alcoholic drink that we've never heard of and will never see again and dance on the tables, let's go really mad this Saturday, and then why don't you stack the fucking car and kill us all? He doesn't recall saying that at all. Now it's Sunday morning and he realises that he has been thinking out loud, shouting into her face, holding her by her bra straps. She says she hates him. The complete bitch psychotic freak hates him.

She says I hate you, do fuck off. She is shaking with anger now, she lights another cigarette with fierce little motions like some kind of military drill. After a while Jamie wanders off and peels the jacket up again to look at Ed. It doesn't even look like him any more. It doesn't look like him at all. His slack upturned face reminds Jamie of raw skinless chicken breasts defrosting by the sink. His open mouth expressing some silent need in the moments before his brain died. Under the sodium light his eyes are looking at nowhere, but like the eyes of a false-backed painting in a cheap horror film they seem to swivel imperceptibly to meet Jamie's gaze no matter what angle he looks at them from.

Lisa thought she'd be practising love yoga with some moronic love monkey that she'd maybe met there by this time. As she sits on the kerb she notices that Jamie has the physique of an eight year old and the face of a paedophile. She decides that she is splitting up with him after they get home. It's not like she's only doing it because she crashed the car. Like she crashed the car so she could break up with him or something. What if she never said anything to him, she reasons, and she died instead of Ed, Jamie therefore never knowing? He would have just gone on living his life as he always had. Except it would be without her, without ever knowing how deeply he was blown out. Or how deeply he would have been in some parallel universe where she made it through the millennium to die of something more interesting than a simple error of judgement leading to an automobile accident.

Her mum assured her that Jamie had nice eyes. She should have sensed that there was a serious problem right at that very moment, when it became clear that Jamie was pulsing on her mother's sexual radar. Her mother, the conservative mother of the future played by a drag queen. That her mother noticed Jamie makes her feel like they are married now, in some way. She can't conceive of that. Laying on the kitchen floor after a heavy night is about as domestic as she gets. Worse still, they sometimes feel like brother and sister. And how sexy is that?

She appears gorgeous to him at the moment, by the light of her Honda Civic. The face full of broken glass look that they're all wearing this season. Tres chic. He can't honestly say he blames her for using the face she carries around on the front of her head to get what she wants. It is after all her only genuine asset.

When she was young, she never did anything even a little bit rebellious. No boyfriends, not really. A virgin until she was nineteen or twenty. He doesn't know that. When he first met her he thought she looked pretty hard. Pretty and hard. Like she drank spirits and stripped for lorry drivers to get her jollies. But she never did anything like that, never even thought about it, just about herself. She thought about the same things as everyone else, had the same kind of life as anyone else might. All night sessions back at somebody's house after all the boozers are shut. Ending up miles away from home, you've forgotten where the car is or even if you had one and can't work out how to get the bus. Talking all night about girls and why do they do that and boys and why don't they do that and self-hatred and life in general, then finally going back to a warm bed and sleeping for eighteen hours. Except tonight. Tonight she drove home.

He doesn't hate himself. He doesn't hate anything. He just thinks everything is funny. There's a big difference. He laughs now, laughs when he thinks of how Lisa said she'd drive because she was the only one who wasn't wasted and Kerry said she'd get out here, don't bother dropping me home because I could do with the walk and it's not like I'm going to get raped or killed or anything har har har and if anyone does try it I can do karate. He doesn't listen to Lisa, who is off on a softly muttered monologue now, interspersed with regularly asking him if he's cold because she's bloody freezing. He talks to himself as well, not really to hear himself talk or to hear the sound of his own voice but just to hear himself think. Lisa, she's always been guarded about being open minded. She doesn't want to know what's in her own head, a born list maker because she's afraid to trust herself to remember things or know anything without having it stuck on the fridge in front of her in black and Post-It note. Mostly she doesn't want to hear what anyone else has to say unless it's of immediate benefit to her. Doesn't care if she feels like she's got nothing in common with most people because she doesn't think she has.

Now Jamie's afloat on a sea of emotion, but he's getting nowhere and feels like throwing up over the side. He spends his weekends with two thousand fucked up E heads who wouldn't know how to be nice to each other or come within six inches of another human being if they weren't drugged up to the eyeballs, completely off their faces and don't know how much is too much. Loved up? Bullshit. Raging now. A load of sordid, rampant quasi-hedonists mauling each other and blurring their minds together until they're the greyish-brown colour of old Plasticene, he thinks. I was out of my box: the excuse for everything from mismatched socks to date rape.

They decide that somebody has to come along soon, after all it's a busy road, and it doesn't occur to either of them to find a phone. Two hours later Lisa is asleep on Jamie's shoulder in a spreading patch of blood. The amount of aspirin she's taken this week to get over last weekend, if you cut her anywhere her blood is bound to spew out like dilute Ribena, lick her and she probably tastes like the inside of a Boots carrier bag. She feels cold, so cold that she seems to radiate it through his clothes like an open fridge. Jamie takes her hands in his and rubs them together.

There is an intense release as she becomes aware of all her blood flowing out of her. Incredible feelings. Agony and sadness mixed up together. Her thoughts are all beaten up and held together with Sellotape. After this she'd like to take a long road trip, in the summer. Not to be scared of cars because of one little mishap. To sleep in the car, live in the car and take odd jobs when she runs out of cash. But nobody ever finds themselves on four wheels around here, be realistic girl child. No epiphanies here. Only the light of a distant all night garage and a burnt out Japanese car on the grass next to an empty road.

Jamie asks her if she's sleeping, five minutes later she says that her eyes are just closed, let's have a silent moment OK? Lisa slurps with the straw against the bottom of the cup and can't remember what flavour the drink was supposed to be. She dedicates several minutes of serious brain power to this enigma, then she tells him to go away because she is going to cry. In fact she is about to fucking weep. He doesn't move. Her teeth are chattering even more than they were before. Cold. Fear. Her watch has stopped because it banged up against the steering wheel. He gave it to her. She doesn't remember him actually doing it. She forgets the exact circumstances. Is that bad? Is that awful? She decides that perhaps forgetting is good.

Jamie's mind wanders and he's thinking of the rich getting richer and everyone else dying, her sticky seeping head in the crook of his arm. Of being a meat puppet on a stick, his arm is going to sleep. Of how it feels to dance and not know of anything but bass and sub-bass, rhythm bulldozing the air. She is so sexy.

115

Lisa waves like a feeble pageant beauty to nobody in particular, then slumps into a sleep which will in time imperceptibly segue into unconsciousness. Her breath on his face smells like coffee and cigarette breath, sort of sour.

The two rows of fuzzy orange lights arc away into the night, erotic and mathematical. Did three men really ask her out tonight like she said? What were they like and what were they thinking about? Were they more like him than not, or less? Were they drive-by bullshitters, university bar rapists? Or were they friendly and cute, so obliging that they would let her stub her smouldering Marlboros out on their smiling little upturned faces? He'd really meant it, the time when he said that she could earn four-and-a-half million pounds, just with the shameless face that she carries around on the front of her head. A come on girl who drinks lorry drivers and strips for spirits but I suppose she knows what she wants, don't we all?

Ed lays in the road, his dirt and blood smudged face half hidden behind a well-worn coat, lonely and deserted. Jamie looks into Lisa's face for a long time, it is covered by darkness and he knows that he will stick to her like napalm. He gently works the watch off of her wrist and onto his, then holds her hand as her pulse ebbs away.

Alistair Gentry was born in 1973. His first novel, *Their Heads Are Anonymous* (Pulp Books, 1997) depicts a bloody coup in an amusement park.

snow baby
catherine johnson

The baby was dead, she knew straight away, stiller than any child, greyer than any child. She pulled back the cotton quilt and lifted her out. There was a slight rememberance of warmth in the tiny body. She held her close hoping some kind of life transference might happen like in a Star Trek film. She sat on the edge of the bed rocking and sobbing until the other child awoke.

"It's ok Lukey, I'm coming."

Then she sat on his bed talking about brains and surgery and sword swallowing. Lukey cuddled his mother and his dead sister, marvelling at the texture of her cool skin, her toothless gums.

"Did someone kill her mum? With a gun?"

"No Lukey love, she just died, babies sometimes do, no one knows why."

"Maybe she didn't like being alive."

"Maybe."

"Do we have to tell the police?"

"Maybe love, maybe."

"Do we have to tell Dad now?"

"In the morning honey."

"It is morning Mum."

It was.

"Your front's wet Mum."

The milk had spread over her t-shirt in two big flower shapes.

"Lyddie's milk," she said looking down. Lyddie lay mouth open in her lap, silver white and slightly sheeny.

Behind the curtains the light was white and fuzzy, early morning February light. Snow had been falling all night, still fell, the big soft slow motion snowflakes that had been falling all week.

She wanted Lyddie to be asleep, just deeply sleeping, like babies sometimes are, heads lolling, mouths open, trails of silver dribble hanging down their fronts, oblivious. She brushed the baby's cheek. Lyddie had gone, at least the breathing Lyddie had gone. She still had her body and it was still perfect.

It was six thirty, soon Dan would be back from work. She sniffed and moved the hair from her face. Luke was jumping off the bed, then walking round to the other side clambering on and jumping off again. She thought of the thump on the kitchen ceiling and the tiny fake snowflakes of plaster drifting down to the lino and settling against the skirting.

"Don't do that love."

"Sorry Mum."

Luke climbed onto the bed and jumped off again.

Lyddie jumped in her arms, but it was only Luke bumping her. She almost laughed.

An hour until Dan came home. What would she say? How could she put it. The tears came suddenly and Luke looked upset.

"I'm OK, really."

She breathed deep to stop the tears, but the breath came shuddery, the gulps of air hitting the back of her mouth and squeezing the tears out of her eyes.

"I'm hungry Mum."

She stood up, wiped the wet from her face and took Luke's hand, "Down we go Lukey," and she felt his soft hot-wet hand in hers and led him downstairs. She held Lyddie upright, the way she liked to be carried, looking back over her shoulder.

The kitchen was north facing, dark, she flicked the light on. "There."

She pushed yesterday's newspaper and the fruit bowl out of the way and lay Lyddie down on her back on the kitchen table.

"She's lovely Mum." Luke smiled.

"She is." She arranged the cotton blanket around her like a cocoon. Lyddie's face and one white fingered hand peeped out. "Like a rosebud."

Luke had Rice Krispies and Weetabix with warm milk, she made herself a cup of coffee, black and heavy and drank it slowly. Luke tipped his bowl up to get at the milk and made a brown sludgy mess on his Action Man pyjamas.

There was a whoosh as the heating came on and the first train rattled across the bridge that cut the little street in half.

She wondered how long Lyddie would be alright, how long before someone, some doctor, some policeman came along and took her away, incinerated her. The thought made her choke.

When Dan comes, she thought, when Dan comes he'll phone

the doctor or the ambulance, and they'll take her away. Lyddie looked happy lying there at the heart of things.

"Shall we change her, Luke, get her out of her jamas?"

Luke nodded and pulled a clean white babygro from where it had been drying on the radiator.

"Here you go."

She held it up, it was so tiny. 'Newborn' said the label, '5kgs.' Lyddie had only made it to 4.9.

"Fetch me a nappy please, Lukey."

He knew the routine, make him helpful, her friends had said, then it won't be so difficult. Luke had never been difficult. Once, one time—the day she went in to have Lyddie—he had cried and cried, held his Mother and refused to let go, wouldn't go to Auntie Clare's.

"Children hate change," Clare said.

People hate change, she thought. She poked Lyddie's limbs into the edges of the babygro as gently as she could, maybe some of her would snap off, rigor mortis. She blanched at the thought of Lyddie's leg hanging off inside the white, white all-in-one. "I'm as bad as you Luke," she said out loud.

Luke wasn't listening, he was licking the Weetabix off the front of his pyjamas. She wanted to wish Dan away, make him never come home, stay here with Luke and Lyddie, frozen like this always. Maybe the roads would be bad and his bus wouldn't run. She lifted the curtain, the garden was white as Lyddie.

She dressed Luke first, pulling on his winter vest and thick Batman socks. "The snow's staying Mum," he said. "Can I go out?"

She looked out beyond the garden, across the roofs of the houses across the road to the white woods that softened the noise from the North Circular. Nothing moved except the snow falling quietly out of thick cloud. It looked so unreal, so fairytale.

"We'll all go out, Lukey." She smiled at Luke. "To the woods." And she dressed, quickly.

She held his frog wellingtons still as he wobbled into them.

And he stamped about the kitchen lino waving his mittens.

"I'll make us a warm drink, Lukey. Warm and white." Then she heated a pan of milk until it frothed almost out of the pan.

"What are you doing Mum?" Luke asked,

"Grating cinnamon, see?" She held some out for him to sniff. "And my special ingredient," she said, pounding the tablets with the sugar to a white sparkly powder. "Like pretend snow."

This had to be the way. She picked up Lyddie in her quilted baby nest and popped the flask into the changing bag. Pulled on Lukey's hat and pushed open the front door.

The cold was fierce outside, and she held Lyddie close.

"We're making the first steps, Mum." Luke scampered in front of her making his steps spiral around. She took close-together steps, careful in case she fell.

"London could be full of wolves, Mum!"

They passed the playground which was still locked and walked up to the fence by the old railway line. This is it, she thought and breathed out quickly, in case she changed her mind.

Luke was catching snowflakes with his mouth, and she almost cried, but she couldn't think of going without him, so put down the bag and smiled at him. Hugged him.

She made a hollow in the snow and lay Lyddie down. The Snow Queen's Baby, she thought. Then she unscrewed the thermos flask and sat down with Lukey and drank the warm white milk.

"We'll sleep in the snow, Lukey, like explorers." Luke smiled.

She thought of the tips of their fingers turning blue-white, like Lyddie's. She hugged them both together, her children asleep in the snow. She watched Luke close his eyes for the last time, kissed him and waited for the tingling cold to transform her.

Catherine Johnson lives in London.
Her 3rd book is out Sept 97 with Women's Press.
She enjoys Fairisle knitting & horseriding.

Another fucking story about drugs and raving and music. All there is to know—the crux of the matter—the important thing, is that any minute now I'm going to turn into my parents. The party is dying; the embers of the top buzz are cooling. I am the sad wanker standing in the hallway, watching everyone leave. Yeah, bye,

HUM

thanks for coming, seeyoulater bye. The lads are already asleep in the upstairs room. They are nice boys, but now they smell of stale beer and farts. I need company, but not that kind. The vodka has split my mind in two and my heart aches. I sit on the stairs for a while, wallowing in my four o'clock in the morning loneliness.

IMPOS

Dawn breaks. Music begins to filter up from the front room. I wander down into the erstwhile dancing arena where the DJ with no name is indulging in some onanistic mixing. He does not see me come in and continues with his work at the decks. He is naked but for his Nikes and his penis stands to attention and bobs to the furious rhythms on the turntables. He is

RHY

whispering sweet nothings to the music going round.

He says:

"<u>Hey baby you can drum my bass any time</u>."

The early morning sun floods the room through the soft focus undulations of the net curtains, and the trees outside convert the light into gods' fingers, which poke the parlour and stroke the DJ with no name. Over the rhythm of the humanly impossible drum sequence, a violin sings and weaves its way into my heart. And the heart aches.

A N L Y

The unknown DJ is still completely engrossed in his solipsistic enjoyment of the decks. Unbeknownst to him, I have made his art obscene. I am a wretched voyeur. Standing there, watching, motionless, without so much as a tap of my foot. Just another fucked wanker soaking up the dregs of a party. The unknown DJ's penis begins to grow to a humanly impossible size and wields its head

S I B L E

over the spinning disc. A girl's voice intones from the speakers—words of a melancholy kind of pornography.

She says: "<u>Love weekender. Why bother, with me? Love weekender</u>."

The cock of the unknown DJ dips, hits the record,

T H M S

rewinds her words, spinning her back, scratching her up until she is made to say:

"<u>Love me— Love me— Love me—</u> "

And my heart aches.

Sophie is 23 and lives in Harlesden. Every other weekend, she performs stories & poems at Monkeys Lounge cabaret in Brighton. She also produces a satirical comic called DJ Bird.

I'm just sitting here, on my own, with the light on and the telly off. It's 12:08am. Too early for the low-flying plane yet. I always hear an aeroplane at about 3 or 4 in the morning, when everything and everyone else is quiet. This drone of a plane breaking through the darkness, giving the night distance and volume — breathing space.

There are loads of planes in the day, but it's noisier anyway, so they just seem like part of every other living thing — normal, mechanical, run-of-the-mill... But at night, they seem more reckless, something to identify with, another living thing in the darkness.

When they're really low, the noise is intensified and it shudders in your chest, like a huge metal cat purring. It feels close. You imagine it crashing into the house...

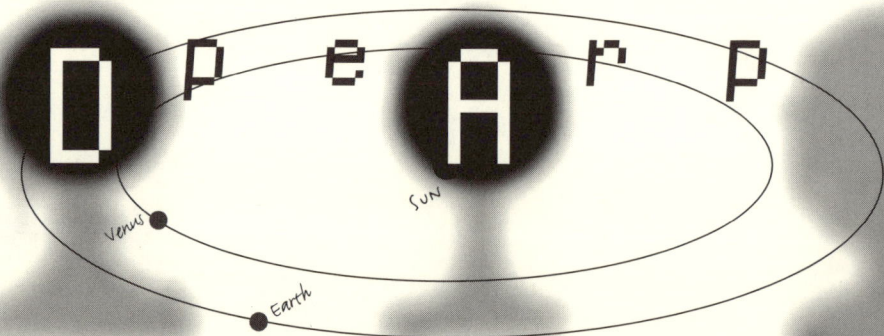

And here one comes, at **12:18**. Not particularly low, not in earshot for long, and you've still got the sound of one or two cars, but still enough to get my attention: The hollow suction sound of the plane and air-turbulence and the noise wavering, going in and out, like a wa-wa guitar noise, not up and down, in and out, as it ricochets, echoes, off the orange-lit townscape of Colchester.

High-pitched buzzing in my ears, like the noise the TV makes when the sound's turned down. An electronic scream. Muscles of neck and base of head are aching with tension. Haemorrhage? Hypochondria...

12:38am. Twenty minutes since the plane? No way! That's the other thing about night — time moves faster. TV on standby. Static electric. Time shifting its arse.

Charlie Crafford

Fragments of life and death and lives splattered randomly across the planet. Like a planet blown apart by a nuclear bomb into a group of asteroids. The asteroids cling to each other, trying to pretend they are still a planet. Is this like family life? Human fragments after being blown apart by a bomb...

Have you ever imagined what it would be like to be blown apart by a bomb? I was in Israel recently. Four bombs in nine days. Bus bombs in Jerusalem. Bomb outside the Dizengoff centre in Tel Aviv killing twelve and injuring about a hundred. The head of the suicide-bomber was found next to the bank, torn from its body.

Your consciousness, centralised in your body, your whole connected body — torso, limbs, head, genitals, all that makes you know for sure that you're you, that aches in the evening after a hectic day — is torn apart and scattered all across a road or shopping-centre.

Imagine your body is your consciousness — each tiny bit of flesh has some consciousness in it, some of what is, or was, you, but is now stuck to the road like hot tar. Sharing the pavement with the ants and the sparrows.

Each piece is still alive, or conscious, but separate. Alive as a new independent body. The whole is dissipated like a dark parody of a human ovum, dividing itself after fertilisation. Flesh molecules on tarmac molecules, fusing, gradually. Starting to chemically react with each other. And the consciousness of the materials fusing into new compounds.

In Israel, after a bomb, Orthodox Jews come along and pick up the bits of human. Dressed in black and white, they scour the street like carrion. They are seen as heroes. Retrieving the flesh for God.

Imagine all those fragments of flesh responding to the same stimulus. Like iron hairs when you pass a magnet over them. Everyday, life follows the Sun around the Earth. Or rather life stays with the Sun, life stays still, and we turn with the Earth, passing in and out of life.

On the way back from Israel, I was sitting next to my girlfriend. Loved up. We were in this plane and dawn was about to break, but it didn't. The sun stayed where it was, just looking out over the horizon, but never completely rising above it.

We must have been travelling at the same speed the Earth turns, causing a perpetual dawn, as we flew over Italy and across Europe. Near the horizon, not far from the sun, was Venus in its Morning Star incarnation. It looked about ten times brighter than any star in a dark sky, and this was twilight.

> The plane powered out of the dark, chasing the dawn, chased by twilight, and we seemed static like the sun. Fixed. Us, the sun, and Venus. The Earth, the flesh of the Earth, below us, was the only thing that moved.

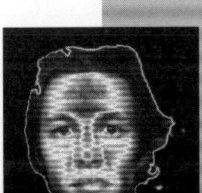

Charlie Crafford was born in 1972, in Colchester, Essex. An ex-raver and apprentice traveller, this is his 1st published work.

ORDER FORM

PULP BOOKS

Call Me	P-P Hartnett	£7.99
Come	Mark Waugh	£8.99
Come + CD	feat. Anti@lias/Overcoat	£11.99
Never Hit The Ground	Kirk Lake	£8.99
Spun Out	Simon Lewis	£8.99
Their Heads Are Anonymous	Alistair Gentry	£8.99

PULP FACTION fiction compilations

5 Uneasy pieces	Cotton, Penrake, Hilaire, McGregor, Tookey	£7.50
Allnighter	Iain Sinclair, Nicholas Blincoe...	£7.50
Random Factor	Jeff Noon, Steve Aylett...	£7.50
Fission	Eroica Mildmay, Alistair Gentry...	£6.99
Technopagan	Jeff Noon, Simon Lewis, Scanner...	£6.99
The Living Room	Deborah Levy, Joe Ambrose...	£6.99
Skin	Barry Adamson, Bertie Marshall...	£5.99

Subtotal

free in the UK
£1 per book Europe
£2 per book rest of world (airmail)

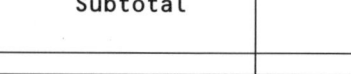 Postage

Orders of 2 books or more deduct £2   ⊖ Multibuy

Name
Address

TOTAL

I enclose a cheque payable to PULP FACTION for £

Send to: **PULP FACTION**, PO Box 12171, London N19 3HB